Praise for the Madis

M000217167

"A sense of danger and menace lightened by Mad's genuine likability and strength. Vallere has crafted an extremely unique mystery series with an intelligent heroine whose appeal will never go out of style."
— *Kings River Life Magazine*

"Instead of clashing, humor and danger meld perfectly, and there's a cliffhanger that will make your jaw drop."
— *RT Book Reviews*

"A terrific mystery is always in fashion—and this one is sleek, chic and constantly surprising. Vallere's smart styling and wry humor combine for a fresh and original page-turner—it'll have you eagerly awaiting her next appealing adventure. I'm a fan!"
— Hank Phillippi Ryan,
Agatha, Anthony, and Mary Higgins Clark Award-Winning Author

"Diane Vallere...has a wonderful touch, bringing in the design elements and influences of the '50s and '60s era many of us hold dear while keeping a strong focus on what it means in modern times to be a woman in business for herself, starting over."
— *Fresh Fiction*

"All of us who fell in love with Madison Night in *Pillow Stalk* will be rooting for her when the past comes back to haunt her in *That Touch of Ink*. The suspense is intense, the plot is hot and the style is to die for. A thoroughly entertaining entry in this enjoyable series."
— Catriona McPherson,
Agatha Award-Winning Author of the Dandy Gilver Mystery Series

"A multifaceted story...plenty of surprises...And what an ending!"
— *New York Journal of Books*

"A humorous yet adventurous read of a mystery, very much worth considering."

— Midwest Book Review

"Make room for Vallere's tremendously fun homage. Imbuing her story with plenty of mid-century modern decorating and fashion tips...Her disarmingly honest lead and two hunky sidekicks will appeal to all fashionistas and antiques types and have romance crossover appeal."

— Library Journal

"If you love Doris Day, you'll love Madison Night, decorator extraordinaire. She specializes in restoring mid-century homes and designs, and her latest project involves abductions, murder and vengeance."

— Books for Avid Readers

"The characters in this series are really great and you laugh and cry along with them when necessary. Madison and Tex are a terrific pair, and the story will definitely keep readers entertained....and after you're done reading you will very much want to find a Doris Day movie to enjoy as much as this book."

— Suspense Magazine

"A charming modern tribute to Doris Day movies and the retro era of the '50s, including murders, escalating danger, romance...and a puppy!"

— Linda O. Johnston,
Author of the Pet Rescue Mysteries

"A well-constructed tale with solid characters and page after page of interesting, intelligent dialogue. Diane Vallere delivers a cunning plot as well as humor and romance."

— ReadertoReader.com

THE
PAJAMA
FRAME

**The Madison Night Mystery Series
by Diane Vallere**

Novels

PILLOW STALK (#1)
THAT TOUCH OF INK (#2)
WITH VICS YOU GET EGGROLL (#3)
THE DECORATOR WHO KNEW TOO MUCH (#4)
THE PAJAMA FRAME (#5)

Novellas

MIDNIGHT ICE

THE PAJAMA FRAME

A Madison Night Mystery

Diane Vallere

LL
HENERY PRESS

Copyright

THE PAJAMA FRAME
A Madison Night Mystery
Part of the Henery Press Mystery Collection

First Edition
Trade paperback edition | February 2018

Henery Press
www.henerypress.com

Trade Paperback ISBN-13: 978-1-63511-300-6
Digital epub ISBN-13: 978-1-63511-301-3
Kindle ISBN-13: 978-1-63511-302-0
Hardcover ISBN-13: 978-1-63511-303-7

Printed in the United States of America

To the DeFelice sisters, Ramona and Annette

ACKNOWLEDGMENTS

I would like to thank the following people for their inspiration, enthusiasm, guidance, and help in bringing *The Pajama Frame* to life: Stanley Donen, Craig Marquis, Jane Feurer, Josh Hickman, the team at Henery Press, and, of course, the real Clara Bixby, without whom there would be no Madison Night (wink).

ONE

"Alice Sweet left me a pajama factory?" I asked in disbelief. In front of me, an abandoned building sat on a neglected plot of land that my Shih Tzu, Rocky, seemed bent on exploring. The building was four stories tall, white, and in serious need of some TLC. Graffiti that had since been painted over was still visible on the lower portion of the exterior. On the upper floors, the damage to the building had been done courtesy of Mother Nature. A cursive "SD" was painted on the front-facing wall by the corner in faded letters that I estimated to be about five feet tall.

"That's what it says in her will," said John, the lawyer who had delivered the news of my latest bizarre inheritance. He opened the leather folio in his hand and read the details on a piece of paper. "Sweet Dreams Pajama Factory goes to Madison Night. When I called the number she left, you answered. You are Madison Night, right?"

"The one and only." I smiled. "But a pajama factory? In downtown Dallas?" I tightened my grip on Rocky's leash while he strained it to sniff the sidewalk that led to the building's entrance.

"Well, it *was* a pajama factory. Now it's an abandoned building. It's been closed for sixty years, so I wouldn't expect too much from the walk-through. It's probably not in the best of shape."

In my line of work, reading the obituaries was good

business practice. Aside from the ick factor, they indicated my next big score. But today's obituaries hadn't given me a lead on inventory for my mid-century modern design business. They'd informed me that a friend had passed away.

Longtime Lakewood resident Alice Sweet died the evening of Feb 10th of natural causes. She was the wife of 1960s sleepwear magnate George Sweet, who died in 1989. She was eighty-six.

Alice Sweet was one of the many women I'd gotten to know from my early-morning swim routine. I shouldn't have been surprised by the obituary; Alice's health had been on the decline in recent months. Eighty-six was a long life by many people's standards, and I sensed she'd had no regrets. During locker room talk, she often shared memories that illustrated she'd been an active participant in her life, not a spectator from the sidelines.

Unlike me, the other women at the pool had little interest in Alice's experience as an extra on the set of *Pillow Talk* back in 1959, or in her mid-century modern time-capsule house that had gone untouched since her husband died in the eighties. Many of them thought Alice's decision to not keep up with the times was silly, but it was the foundation for our friendship. She'd always promised I'd have first pick of her belongings when she passed away. That was of little consolation now.

I had torn the obituary page from the paper and set it aside. Mad for Mod, my interior-decorating business, thrived because I had an inside track to original fixtures and decorative objects d'art. That track had been established through unlikely friendships with the local funeral parlors and lawyers who managed estates. It wasn't unusual for me to place a call after reading an obit like Alice's, to find out the contact information for the next of kin and make an offer to take the entire estate off their hands. For the first time since I'd started using this practice, the gesture felt sleazy. Even if Alice had indicated she wanted her belongings to go to me, I didn't want to benefit from her move to the great mid-mod classic in the sky.

As it turned out, Alice had taken the ick factor out of the equation by naming me in her will, a gesture that was only slightly more awkward since the lawyer by my side was also her grandson.

John Sweet, said lawyer, wore a gray suit, white shirt, and yellow tie. His brown hair had a faint orange cast to it that suggested his natural color was more salt-and-pepper. It was neatly cut and combed away from his face, and his brushed-steel framed glasses stood out against his skin. When I'd arrived at the pajama factory, he'd scanned my outfit in about the same amount of time it had taken me to scan his.

Today I wore a pair of light blue narrow ankle pants, a matching cropped blazer, and white canvas Keds sneakers. Under the jacket was a yellow turtleneck. My blonde hair was pulled into two low ponytails. My coloring was fair naturally, but four times a year I had a blonde rinse that perked up the subtle ashy shade that came with each passing birthday. A month ago, I'd turned forty-nine, and I was starting to wonder what delightful physical issues would accompany the changing tone of my hair. I'd recently had bangs cut, which I wasn't sure fit on a woman my age. There are those who might argue that a woman my age probably shouldn't wear yellow and aqua, or ponytails, either. You could make a case for the fact that I didn't care what people thought of how I looked, and you'd be right.

"I'm still confused. In all the time we spent together, Alice never mentioned a pajama factory. The contents of her house, including her wardrobe, yes. Are you sure this is right?"

"That's what it says in her will," John said.

"Why didn't she ever tell me about it?"

"I can't answer that. My grandfather owned the Sweet

Dreams Pajama Company in the fifties. The company closed before I was born. The only evidence we had that it ever existed was what seemed like an unlimited supply of old-fashioned pajamas."

"You didn't know she still owned it until she came to see you?"

"No. I assumed it had been repossessed by the bank. It's been sitting here vacant where the residents are mostly four-legged and eat out of the trash. Another factory in the neighborhood was converted into apartments in the late nineties, but it's rare to make something like that work. Under normal circumstances, you'd have to clear the taxes on the property before taking ownership, but she said in the will that she has an escrow account to pay that money, so once all the paperwork is filed, you'll get the building free and clear." He paused for a moment. "I'm guessing the explanation is inside the letter she left you."

I turned to face him. "You didn't say anything about a letter."

"It's at the office with the will. I expected you to meet me there."

"I don't always do the expected thing when it comes to the death of a friend." I managed a smile. "Maybe we can go there now."

Despite our attempts to keep things light, neither John nor I were in celebratory moods.

Even before meeting John, I knew he considered Alice's blue living room and pink bathroom a joke. Her husband, George, had been married once before Alice, and the children and grandchildren from that marriage had been raised as her own. But her husband had died almost thirty years ago, and she'd never wanted to redecorate.

Thirty years. While I stared at the long-abandoned building

in front of me, I did the math. Alice had been fifty-four when she found herself widowed and on her own again. Only five years older than I was now. Maybe that's why she had always felt like a kindred spirit even though she was from a different generation. She'd discovered her new independence late in life too.

In my experience, families like Alice's—estranged and merely putting up with Mom's "quirky desire" to not change with the times—usually sold property off to the top bidder. These days that was through a house flipper. He'd come along, gut the place, toss her pink toilet and tub into the nearest landfill and slap together a bare-bones renovation. All signs of Alice would be gone. And while logically I knew there was just as much of a chance that the house flipper would be a woman, I refused to believe a woman could be as cold-hearted as a man when it came to demolishing a pink bathroom.

I made no move to get closer to the building. Despite the seemingly generous nature of the inheritance, I was flummoxed. This was most definitely not the same as rescuing a pink bathroom. "I don't know what to say. This is—this is completely unexpected." I tore my attention away from the building and faced John again. "What happens next?"

John stared at me for a few seconds before speaking. "Full disclosure, Ms. Night, Grandma Alice and I weren't that close. When she came to my law firm, she already drafted a will. That was the first time I'd seen her in over a decade. Her health was declining, and she asked me if I would handle her estate when she died. I think it was her way of trying to make amends. I always assumed, even though we weren't close, that whatever she had would go to the family. Your name popping up took me by surprise. The fact that it's more than a couple of items from her closet makes me want to know you more, to know how you were able to forge a relationship with her when my family couldn't."

The whole situation tamped down any emotional response I had to Alice's death and forced me to think objectively. I pretended we weren't talking about a friend of mine who had died, but a business transaction, and channeled the same emotional detachment I'd relied on in the past when faced with situations like this. I considered the request and quickly concluded that, if it had been my own parents, I'd probably be asking the same questions.

"When I first moved to Dallas, I was recovering from a knee injury, and my doctor suggested daily swimming would be the best physical therapy. I've always been a morning person, and after fighting the crowds at the pool at various times of the day, I discovered six a.m. was the best time for me to schedule my swim. I don't know if you've ever spent time at a pool at six a.m., but you'll find that the majority of the other swimmers are retirees. Alice was among a group of women in their eighties who swam at the same pool I do each morning, and that's how we met."

John nodded. "I do remember she loved swimming. My dad said Grandma used to compete when she was growing up."

I smiled. "Alice must have felt comfortable in that world long after she stopped competing. It was a social thing for her and her friends. They swam laps, but at their age, it was more about camaraderie with each other. The women would giggle and poke fun at the men and sometimes tell stories about old boyfriends."

I remembered how they'd reacted the day police Lieutenant, now Captain, Tex Allen, had joined me in my daily routine. Until that day, the only companion I'd brought to the pool had been my Shih Tzu, and having a physically fit policeman thirty years their junior show up with me had triggered the kind of girl talk I didn't think a grandson should hear. I smiled to myself, and then, when I saw him looking at me, forced the smile off my face and continued. "I was new in town. I didn't know anybody. Your grandma and her friends accepted me into their circle."

"You were a surrogate daughter to her," he said. He didn't seem happy about the observation.

"No, I wasn't." I waved my hands up and down my vintage pantsuit. "This is how I dress every day. I wear what they wore, and I reminded them of who they were before they got old. I think they saw me as one of them who had somehow made use of a time machine."

John's forehead wrinkled in consternation. I continued, "John, your grandmother told me she planned to leave me her clothes and her furniture because she knew I would wear the clothes and find the furniture a new home with someone who loves that style of decorating as much as she did. I can't pretend to know why she left me this building. All I can think is that she might have thought, after all this time, having you deal with the factory would leave you with a big pain in the butt that you would resent."

John relaxed. He looked down at his hands. When he looked back up, there were tears in his eyes. "That makes sense," he said. "I was afraid she'd been haunted by the rumors all these years and wanted you to do something about proving them wrong."

I tensed, a counter-reaction to John's apparent relief. "What rumors?"

"I guess if you didn't know about the factory, then you wouldn't know about the rumors." He looked up at the façade of the building for a few moments and then looked at me. "Sweet Dreams Pajama Factory was once a thriving business, but after what happened, Grandpa had no choice but to close it and walk away."

John tipped his head down, and I found it hard to read the expression on his face. "Do you mean the war?" I asked. "I would have thought a factory would thrive after World War II ended and soldiers came home."

"That's what should have happened, but it was something else. One of the pajama models died in a freak accident inside the factory. My granddad closed down production and took a job as a traveling salesman, and it's been sitting vacant ever since."

"That's horrible," I said. "But what are the rumors you mentioned?"

"There were rumors that my grandfather was having an affair with the model and that the accident wasn't an accident at all. That's why the building's been closed. To a whole lot of people, it's not just an abandoned building. It's also a crime scene."

TWO

I gasped. "Alice never mentioned a word about that. How common are the rumors?"

John chose to answer a question I hadn't asked. "On one hand, I would have thought if you two were friends, she would have told you about the whole ordeal. On the other hand, I can see why she wouldn't talk about it. Grandma Alice was my grandpa's second wife. His first wife, my real grandmother, died of cancer. Grandpa wasn't around much when I was growing up because he was on the road. My dad used to say he took that job so he wouldn't have to hear what people were saying."

"But if that was sixty years ago, surely the rumors would have been long forgotten by now."

"Right? You would think. But people don't want to let this one die." He gestured toward the building. "When I was drawing up the will, Alice gave me a list of special-interest groups that want it. I have it at the office. If you don't want to deal with the building either, you could probably sell it to one of them."

"What kinds of groups?" I asked suspiciously. Already it sounded like opportunists were sniffing around Alice's possessions. Developers who would knock down the building and aforementioned house flippers that would level her house— the bane of my mid-mod existence.

"The Historical Preservation Society of Dallas is one of them."

"The HPSD? But they do good work. Why do they want to

knock down the pajama factory?"

John looked at me like he'd missed something. "They don't want to knock it down. They're petitioning for it to have historical designation."

"That's good, right?"

"I thought so too, but Alice told them she wasn't interested. It's your decision now."

I looked back at the building. Already there was more here than met the eye, and not just because the building had been sealed for sixty or so years.

"Madison, did Alice ever talk about my granddad? Or about our family?"

"No. We talked mostly about her days as an extra on the set of *Pillow Talk*, and how she decorated the living room."

I'd first met Alice during the early morning swim hours at Crestwood pool. My physical similarities to the singer-actress-dancer Doris Day were obvious, made even more so by my second-hand 1950s/1960s wardrobe. When Alice had commented on it and I told her about my lifelong love of Doris Day, she immediately abandoned her water aerobics class and joined me on the pool deck. My decorating studio opened two hours late that day because I hadn't been able to tear myself away from Alice's stories.

I didn't know what John was looking for, but if he needed me to validate his relationship with his grandmother, I wasn't going to lie. The one thing she did tell me was that her family said she lived in the past. Alice didn't treat me like the daughter she didn't have; she treated me like an equal. *That's* why we were friends.

"You really don't have any idea why she left this to you?"

I shook my head. "Maybe we should head back to your office and take a look at that letter."

* * *

The offices of Stanley & Abbott were located just outside the beltway on the northeast side of Dallas toward Garland. I made good time and arrived before John. I expected a sleek, impersonal building with valet parking and security attendants. Instead, I found a small red brick ranch that had been converted from a residence to a place of business. Two cars sat in the lot: a white van and a shiny coupe. I parked in one of the visitor spaces and led Rocky, my Shih Tzu, to the door.

"Do you know anything about printers?" asked a harried older man behind a mahogany desk. He wore suit pants and a blue dress shirt with the sleeves rolled up. He held a syringe filled with dark liquid in one hand. His fingers were stained with ink, and a pile of papers with a varying assortment of fingerprints lay scattered on the surface of the desk in front of him. In the background, the sound of a vacuum cleaner came from an office down the hall.

I looped Rocky's leash around the back of the chair that faced the desk and gently pushed the man out of the way. I took the syringe and scanned the desk for the empty ink cartridge.

"It fell," he said.

I bent down and found the small plastic container under the credenza. Using a ruler from the desk, I corralled it out from under the furniture and then found the opening on top where the syringe fit. A few seconds later, the cartridge was newly filled and back in the printer. I released a paper jam from the back, fed new paper into the unit, and printed a test page.

"You're hired," the man said.

"I'm not here for a job."

"Oh?" He looked behind me and then refocused on me. "Your name isn't Gladys, is it?"

"Do I look like a Gladys?"

He wiped his hands on a few more blank pages of printer paper and then made no secret of the fact that he was judging me by my vintage pantsuit and newly cut bangs. "You look a little like a Gladys."

I guess I did. "I'm Madison Night." I held out my hand, and then, thinking twice about the stains on his, withdrew. He didn't seem offended.

"I'm Mr. Stanley." He smiled. "Always wanted a secretary named Gladys. Seems like the name of a real go-getter, don't you think?"

"Um, sure."

"No bother. Madison is a fine name too." He sat down. "May I ask what brings you here?"

"I'm a client. John Sweet arranged to meet me at his grandmother's property."

The sound of the vacuum switched off, and a dark-haired woman appeared in the hallway. The name "Frannie" was embroidered on her smock. She saw the ink fingerprints on the sides of the printer and pulled a spray bottle and a rag off her cleaning cart and set to work removing them.

I turned my attention back to Mr. Stanley, whose face appeared flushed. "Why did you meet John at Alice's house? Are you interested in her property?" he asked.

"John wanted to talk to me about an inheritance. He said he's executing Alice's will."

"That can't be. We're tax lawyers, not estate planners."

While the white-haired law partner and I shared a moment of confusion, the cleaning woman picked up a stack of ink-stained papers and moved them to the trash. She pulled the plastic trash bag out of the bin, knotted the top shut, and added it to a much bigger trash bag on the bottom of her cart.

"Excuse me, Mr. Stanley," she said. "I'm all done for today."

"Thank you, Frannie. See you Wednesday."

Frannie handed Mr. Stanley a ring of keys, which he dropped into his pocket. His eyes never left my face. When Frannie was gone, Mr. Stanley reached forward and tapped the spacebar on the computer. When the screen woke up, he hit Control C. "Hmmm, that's interesting."

"What?"

"John has your name on the office calendar, but he didn't provide information about your client needs. Maybe we should start at the beginning."

"I'm starting to think there is no beginning. I'm sorry to have wasted your time."

"On the contrary. It's been a pleasure." He smiled like he was thinking about a pleasant memory he didn't share. "Besides, you saved me from committing inkicide." He held up his ink-stained hands.

"You wouldn't be convicted," I said. "Your cleaning woman just discarded the evidence." I pulled a packet of Handi Wipes out of my bag and handed him one. He looked at them like a five-year-old might look at a surprise candy bar.

"Are you sure you don't want to be my secretary? I offer a competitive wage."

"I'm a decorator. I think I'm better suited to fixing your empty wall space than your files."

I meant it as a joke, but Mr. Stanley's face fell. "We've had seventeen secretaries since Mr. Abbott and I started the firm. Sixteen of them were women. I hired John two years ago. Thought I was being modern by hiring a man for a woman's job" —he appeared to take note of my possibly disapproving expression and backpedaled—"Not a woman's job. A job that had, up to that point, been held by women." He leaned back and tapped his fingers on the desk. "I'm an old dog trying to learn new tricks. John and I had our differences when he first came to work here, but we settled into a working relationship. I'm sure he'd prefer a different title, but after seventeen years of calling them secretaries, it seemed sexist to call him something different."

"Interesting argument, but then again, you are the lawyer."

"Tax lawyer. I don't get into a lot of arguments with the IRS." He picked a business card off the desk and held it out to me. "Tell your boss to consider us come tax time."

"You just did." He looked at me like he didn't know what I meant. "I'm the boss. I own my own decorating company, Mad for Mod." I stepped backward. "If soap and water don't take that ink off your hands, try hairspray."

The door to the law firm swung open, and John came in. "You're already here," he said, slightly out of breath. "I thought it would take you longer."

"John, did you represent yourself as an estate planner to this woman?" Mr. Stanley asked.

"No, sir."

"Yes, you did," I said.

John turned back to me. "You inferred that. All I told you was that Alice Sweet left you a factory and a sealed letter, and I wanted to meet with you to discuss them. I told you I had the information at the law firm. This is a law firm, is it not?"

I thought about our meeting on the street, the questions I'd asked, and his brief explanation about why he'd been appointed the executor of the will. Regardless of the job title John held at Stanley & Abbott, he appeared to have picked up a thing or two about misdirection.

Mr. Stanley stood up. "John, why did you lead Ms. Night on?"

John's face colored. "I needed to talk to her, and I didn't know how else to make sure she'd meet me."

Mr. Stanley turned to me. "I'm sorry, Ms. Night. We're not in the practice of tricking potential clients to come to us for appointments."

"Wait!" John said. He put his hand up to stop me from leaving. "I promise I can explain everything. You're already here. You know about the factory. Mr. Stanley, can we use conference room B? I blocked it out for the afternoon."

"This isn't your private clubhouse. We run a business here. Those conference rooms are for clients."

"Mr. Stanley, my grandmother came to me with a will she'd drawn up on her own. She wanted me to make it legal. I told her we weren't that kind of law firm, but she didn't care. She said it was very important to her that she give us her business. I've been taking night courses in estate planning, and I had my professor check my work. All of the paperwork is in order."

"If it's all the same to Ms. Night, I'd like to sit in on this meeting," Mr. Stanley said. He looked at me.

John looked at me too. I'd spent the morning learning about Alice's pajama factory, and the desire to know more about that outweighed the awkwardness of having been tricked. "If it was fine with Alice, it's fine with me," I said.

The four of us (three people plus Rocky) moved from the lobby to a conference room. It was as expected: dark wood walls and a dark wood table surrounded by dark leather chairs. A pitcher of water sat on a tray in the middle of the table next to four upside-down cut crystal glasses. Condensation from the pitcher had pooled onto the interior bed of the tray, leaving the glasses themselves in a floaty puddle of water.

John flipped the glasses over one by one, shook the water off, and then filled them. For the person who had called the meeting, he seemed more nervous than I would have expected. I sipped my water and waited for the show to begin.

"I suppose I could have been a little clearer. Madison, as I told you, Alice Sweet was my grandmother. Step-grandmother, I guess would be the better term. My granddad was George Sweet, but my real grandmom—my mom's mom—was his first wife. Alice contacted me a few months ago and asked if I could help her with a will. It's not what we do, but she said she specifically wanted me to handle it."

"That sounds like Alice," I said.

Mr. Stanley leaned forward and kept his eyes on John for a few seconds. He tapped his palm on the highly polished wood table. "I volunteered to sit in on this meeting to act as your advisor. John's relationship with the deceased could give the appearance of impropriety to our firm, and by me sitting in, we're going to make sure everything is done to the letter. Isn't that right, John?"

John tried, unsuccessfully, to mask his displeasure at Mr. Stanley's presence. He nodded his assent but tucked his head, keeping his reddening face obscured. He pulled a thick padded envelope out from the folder. It had my name written across the front. "Maybe this will provide some answers."

I took the envelope. "Do I have to open this now?"

John looked like he was about to speak, but Mr. Stanley held his hand palm-side out, and John remained quiet.

Mr. Stanley turned to me. "Your inheritance is not contingent upon what is in the letter. The fact that it's sealed tells me it's of a personal nature, and based on the circumstances, I'm going to advise you to open it in private. If you choose to share the information at that time, that's your decision."

I looked at the envelope. I'd never had reason to see Alice's handwriting, but it looked exactly like I would have expected. Neat and cursive, the style that was taught in grade school long before computers were standard issue. I pictured a young Alice in class, looping her A and practicing how to write the rest of the letters of her name at precisely the same height.

I tucked the envelope into my handbag. "John, I respect

that Alice was your relative, but I'd rather open this at home," I said. "I hope you understand."

The rest of my time at Stanley & Abbott was spent signing paperwork and waiting while copies of my ID were made on the same multi-functional printer that had given Mr. Stanley such trouble when I'd first arrived. Rocky sat by my feet, tired and listless. He looked up at me without moving his head for a moment, and then lifted his paw and swatted at the laces on my sneakers. I held my hand down. He sniffed it and then turned his head the other way as if he just couldn't be bothered.

After finishing up with the paperwork, I checked that Alice's letter was secure in my handbag and then left. It was after eight and the sun was setting. Rocky, normally well behaved in the passenger seat of my Alfa Romeo, grew antsy and walked over my lap to stare out the window. It was growing darker by the minute, and traffic wasn't looking good. I pulled out of the lot, through the neighborhood, and headed home.

A few years ago, I'd acquired a two-bedroom house for the low price of the back taxes. It was slightly more involved than that, but the end result was that I moved from a one-bedroom unit in an apartment building to a split-level house with a detached garage. I still—and would probably always—refer to the place as Thelma Johnson's house, the original owner. Being entrenched in decades past for both business and pleasure gave me a disproportionate tendency toward keeping said past alive.

Thelma Johnson's house was in a section of Dallas referred to as the M streets: Munger, Mockingbird, Morningside, etc. I turned from Gaston to Monticello and drove to the corner plot with a separate garage. I'd taken to using the garage for an overflow of inventory and had even built a rudimentary workbench for minor repairs to garage-sale finds. The space where my car could have gone was currently occupied with a large wooden printing press I'd found abandoned on a street corner during one of my early morning walks. Getting it back here had been a bit tricky.

I parked my car parallel to the stretch of shrubbery by the mailbox, and Rocky and I got out of the car. Rocky peed on a tomato plant and left a stinkier deposit by the base of the Japanese maple tree. Somewhat lighter, he trotted to the sidewalk and picked up a stuffed turtle in his mouth. He returned to the garden, dug a hole, and dropped the turtle inside. I wasn't sure when the burying phase had begun, but in the past few months, I'd discovered various toy appendages jutting out from the perimeter of the garden. Each time I dug them out, washed them thoroughly, and returned them to his toy bin. For some reason, he was more determined to bury the turtle than any of the others.

I unlocked the front door, and Rocky ran inside. He waited while I locked it and unlocked the door on the other side of the solarium that opened into the kitchen. He ran toward his water bowl. I dropped my handbag and keys onto the colorful tablecloth and fished out the sealed envelope from Alice. My curiosity had been idling on the back burner long enough. I slid a vintage letter opener under the corner of the envelope and sliced through the paper. The letter was written in the same careful cursive script as on the envelope.

Dear Madison, it started.

You may be surprised by my decision to leave you my husband's pajama factory. I wish I could have seen your face when you heard! But if you're reading this, then my number has been called. I have no regrets about how I lived my life. I died a happy woman, having deeply loved two different men before discovering the pleasure of singlehood. I suspect you know how that feels.

As for Sweet Dreams, I was forced to make a choice. In my family, a black cloud hangs over the building. You may have heard there are rumors that go hand in hand with my husband's pajama factory. I never spoke of them for fear that if I did, they'd be proven true. But I was aware of them, and while I had no interest in proving whether they were true or false, they were part of my life. I saved articles about the factory and locked them in a unit at Hernando's Hide-It-Away Storage Facility. The key is in this envelope. Should you choose to uncover the truth, you have my blessing.

THREE

When I started reading, I'd expected an explanation of sorts, or possibly even an inventory list of items Alice was giving me and what they'd meant to her. That was how she'd thought. Nothing was simply an item. Her salt and pepper shakers were Holt-Howard Cozy Kitties that her husband had brought back from a business trip to New York in 1960. He'd walked directly into the Manhattan Gift Center on Fifth Avenue and picked them out from an assortment of charming animals. Her vintage chrome Sunbeam toaster with radial control was a wedding present—she'd received two of the same gift and instead of returning one, had kept it in reserve for when the first one broke down. Even her wardrobe was more than a closet of clothes: the suit she wore when she met Jackie Kennedy, the pedal pushers she had on the day she ran into James Coburn in the grocery store, the hat she bought with her rent money after seeing Vera Miles try it on at Neiman Marcus. Her stories could have been made up purely for my entertainment, but I loved the way her eyes lit up when she told them, so I'd always believed she was telling me as it had been.

But this wasn't a closet of old clothes or even a collection of salt and pepper shakers. Alice hadn't given me an inventory. She'd given me something far more important. Even before I extracted a key from the corner of the envelope, I understood Alice's gift to me was for both of us. For all of her stories about the life she'd lived, she'd kept one pretty large secret. And now, she'd tasked me with uncovering the truth that she'd been unable to face. To clear her husband's name and give her family a legacy.

I kept reading.

It's often easier to believe what we want than what is true, and that was my choice. But these last few months, I've looked at things differently. Sweet Dreams employed a lot of young women who needed to work to support their families during the war. They were the heart and soul of the company, and without them, Sweet Dreams wouldn't have had a nightie to sell. I believe my husband George did something great when he employed a generation of women who had never considered working in a factory, and I believe there are hundreds of families scattered around Dallas who benefitted from the dedication those women had to the company when their men were fighting overseas. The truth can no longer hurt me.

You're a talented young decorator who has the power to turn the building into something fresh and new. I wouldn't "dream" of telling you what to do with it, but I know you will give your decision great thought and that's why I consider you a true friend. Whatever you decide, you won't be able to do it by yourself. Ask that cute fella who's always hanging around you for help.

Speaking of which, there's something you need to be told, and I've always prided myself on speaking the truth to my friends. You're my friend, so here goes: your past is no more important than your future. I watched you come to terms with several difficult things since we've met, and I know you're a different person because of those incidents. But beware the prison you build. Life is short, and you should not leave opportunities on the

table that you will regret. Take that as you will.
   Sincerely, Alice

I heard Alice's voice in my head as I read her words. She felt so close, like she was in the room, brewing a cup of coffee or a mug of tea. I felt her presence around me, a comforting glow. I wanted to believe she was there. And in that moment, I knew I would not sell the factory, and I would not share the contents of the letter with her grandson, John. My relationship with Alice was something for me to cherish and protect and that's exactly what I wanted to do.

I held the tarnished key up to the light. A piece of tape had been attached to the base of the key with #185 written on it. The storage facilities were long since closed, and while a new sense of excitement filled me, I'd have to wait until morning to discover the history of the factory. I added the key to my keyring and turned in for the night.

The next morning, I woke at five thirty. I pulled on a bathing suit and stepped into a terrycloth dress that buttoned down the front and then stuffed underwear and a change of clothes into a bag. Rocky seemed content to sleep on the bed, so I kissed him on the head and drove to the Gaston Swim Club. I much preferred the outdoor Crestwood pool, but until Memorial Day my morning swims would take place in an overly chlorinated indoor pool with a snooty lifeguard and barely supervised doggie daycare.

I parked and went inside, stashed my bag in a locker, and carried my cap, goggles, and towel to the deck. The usual suspects, friends of Alice, joined me at the end of the lane. I tucked my blonde hair under my cap and returned the same feeble smile they offered me. Without words, we shared our grief but jumped into the pool and started to swim. It was like as long as we did what we did every day, nothing had changed. If only life was as easy to swallow as an unexpected mouthful of chlorinated water.

As usual, my workout lasted longer than the octogenarians'. My laps had started in turmoil, propelled clumsily by the need to physically deal with the stress of losing a friend. By the time an hour was up, my muscles had loosened. I finished my last lap with a rare enthusiasm for the day. As I climbed out of the water and stood on the deck, voices floated to me from the locker room.

"What do you think will happen to it?" asked one.

"I don't know. It's been sealed all these years. Alice wouldn't allow them to search it, but who knows now?"

"It's a shame she even had to deal with that. George was a good husband and a provider, all the way up to his death."

"That's not what I heard."

"Oh?"

It was human nature to gossip, and there was no doubt what the women were talking about. Only believers in the deceased's ability to spy on the living would consider whether or not Alice could hear them, and judging from the conversation that carried to me, the women in the locker room must have believed Alice was still negotiating the plane between life and death and had more important things to deal with than their chit chat. And while it might seem strange how willing they were to talk about her, I knew this was how the ladies of the pool dealt with the death of one of their own. Talking about Alice was a way of keeping her in the here and now.

I joined them in the locker room. "Madison," Grace said, "we were just talking about Alice."

"The pool won't feel the same without her," I said.

"Do you think she'll keep her promise to leave you her

wardrobe?"

"She left me more than her wardrobe. She left me her pajama factory." My news got the proper response from Grace. I told her what little I knew but left out details of Alice's letter. The other women continued to dress, but their shift to silence in place of the gossip I'd heard from outside told me there was more to the story than I knew.

I showered off the chlorine and dressed in an orange textured Orlon two-piece dress with three-quarter sleeves. Ivory arrow tabs by the collar and hem provided whimsical detail. I pulled on ivory tights and slipped my feet into lime green Keds, dawdling until all but one woman remained with me. Her name was Clara Bixby. At ninety-four, she was the oldest of the swimmers at the Gaston Swim Club. Her attendance wasn't as regular as the others, but I was impressed by her dedication to working out all the same.

Clara stood in front of the mirror arranging her white cap of hair into a soft style that framed her face. I joined her and finger-combed my own hair and then gave up and used a brush. We stood side by side, primping in similar ways. Clara pulled out a coral lipstick and swiped it on and then pursed her lips at the mirror. The action made me giggle.

She held up the lipstick. "Revlon Fire and Ice," she said in a slow Texas drawl that belied her heritage. "I was twenty-four when the ads for this came out, and I thought the model in the pictures was the most glamorous person I'd ever seen. I ran out and bought as many tubes of the lipstick I could afford and kept them in my refrigerator. Used to dye my hair black like hers too, but I gave that up."

"It's good to have a signature lipstick," I said. "Empowering. And there's probably a whole cult of women who would pay top dollar for your Fire and Ice." I pulled a tube of lipstick out of my handbag. "I'm a 'Cherries in the Snow' lady myself."

We shared a smile. I didn't usually go for red lipstick in the middle of the day, but it was a bonding moment, so I dabbed it on. I pursed my lips like she had, and she laughed.

"I heard you tell Grace that Alice left you Sweet Dreams. You know, I worked there before it closed," she said.

"You worked at Sweet Dreams?"

"Right there on the factory floor. I was responsible for sleeves." She tucked her lipstick back into her handbag. "It was during the war. My daddy was off fighting, and all us girls pitched in to help Mamma out. Two-fifty an hour, forty hours every week. There were three of us. I was the oldest. I was just seventeen years old."

Clara charmed me with her gentle accent and her references to her mamma and daddy. Even at ninety-four, I could see her younger self shining below the surface. There was a pride in her when she spoke of working. She was an honest-to-god Rosie the Riveter, except her tool of trade had been a sewing machine. She was one of the women who had advanced feminism decades before the movement grew legs in the sixties.

"Did Alice tell you anything about the factory?" she asked.

I thought of the letter and the promise of newspaper clippings at Hernando's Hide-It-Away, but until I knew anything for sure, I kept that to myself. "She hinted at a few things but said the decision of what to do with the building is up to me. I admit I was completely surprised. Alice told me about her decorating choices on every inch of her house, but she never mentioned the pajama factory. I didn't even know that was her husband's line of business until I read her obituary."

"Do you know about what happened there?"

"I've heard a little gossip, but that's all. I was hoping to do some research on it today. But if you worked there, I'd love to hear your stories."

Clara grew somber. "Even after all this time, it's hard for me to talk about those days. That factory changed my life in more ways than I can count."

"It must have been hard for you when George Sweet went out of business."

"He didn't have much choice. After my sister died, the scandal surrounding her death surely would have caused more problems than he could handle."

"Your sister?"

"Yes," she said. "My younger sister Suzy was the pajama model who died in the accident."

FOUR

Clara watched me in the reflection of the mirror. We stood side by side, two fair haired women in red lipstick that now appeared far too cheerful for the sudden mood shift in the locker room.

"I'm so sorry," I said. I put my hand on her forearm in a consoling gesture. "I respect your desire to keep those memories personal."

"That's just the thing," she said. "It's been a long time since I worked there and my memory isn't what it once was. I've outlived my parents and my sisters and what little I do remember from those days is going to die with me. Alice never talked about the factory, but the fact that she left it to you says she didn't believe the rumors. That building was once a vibrant place of business. It's been shut up all these years, but not because Alice didn't have plenty of offers on it."

"I heard there were people who thought the building should be unsealed and searched for new evidence in your sister's death."

"Alice and I never talked about the factory, as you can imagine. But every once in a while, someone would stir up talk. I've never cared much for beating around the bush, so I told her I didn't hold her responsible for what happened to my sister. I never saw George do anything untoward in the time I worked there, and I'd be more surprised to find out he was guilty than to find out he was innocent. Still, there's one way to shut down the rumors."

"Unseal the building and see if the rumors are true," I said, coming to the same conclusion.

"As Alice told you, it's your choice now," she said. She squeezed my hand, smiled, and left.

My curiosity level over the pajama factory had risen since being there last night. I drove home and threw my wet towel and terrycloth clothes in the dryer and collected Rocky. The early hour meant commuter traffic. Highway 75 had been under construction since I'd moved to Dallas five years ago, and it showed no signs of completion. I stuck to Greenville Avenue as long as I could, crossed over Gaston, and turned right on Columbia. About half an hour after I left, I pulled into a visitor space in front of the vacant factory. A small part of me wished I had a key, but a much larger part questioned what Pandora's box I'd open once I unsealed those doors.

Sweet Dreams sat abandoned on the western side of the highway in what could best be described as an industrial park in the Deep Ellum part of town. On the eastern side stood the Adam Hats Lofts, a former automotive plant turned hat factory that had found a third reincarnation as a complex of trendy loft apartments. On the west was the now abandoned Union Bankers building, once the Pythian Temple, that had been left to ruin shortly after achieving historic designation. Those two properties represented everything I'd come to learn about Dallas since moving here. Its deep, varied history was there for the world to see if they wanted, but whether the focus was on the run-down, ignored elements or the hip, trendy ones was up to the viewer.

I hadn't spent much time in Deep Ellum. It was mostly known for its nightlife, and being a morning person in her late forties, the idea of "nightlife" was a vague concept, not a practice. Looking around, I figured the nightlife was a pale imitation of what it had once been. Pre-World War II, "the war" both Alice and Clara had referred to, had been fertile ground for jazz and blues musicians. The decade that followed was when the factory was running, when Clara had her first job, and when Suzy, her sister, had died.

In the morning light, the buildings in the neighborhood looked cold and uninviting. I wondered what it must have been like then, to work alongside people who you met because of circumstance and befriended out of convenience. Had the employees ever left work and gone out together? Had those early female workers been treated with respect or had they struggled to establish their place in a traditionally male world? Had there been office romances? Had the employees lobbied for raises like in *The Pajama Game*?

I thought about the rumors surrounding the pajama model's death and Alice's husband George. It wasn't unlikely for a relationship to spring up between people who worked together, but I didn't want to believe the worst.

John Sweet had said something yesterday, something in passing that stuck with me. Special-interest groups had been after Alice to get possession of the building. I now understood why she would have turned them down.

Whispered rumors would have become sensationalized news stories. George Sweet's reputation would have been in question. Alice, who had spent the past thirty years on her own with a network of friends, would have been relegated back into the role of wife of a former sleepwear magnate. Plus, once the building was unsealed, there would be the problem of ongoing security. It made perfect sense that she'd left well enough alone.

But she left it to me to do otherwise. If I intended to do anything with the building, I would have to unseal it first, and there was no way to avoid the outcome. And for Alice's sake, I wasn't going to ignore the difficulties that came with my decision.

My phone rang from the depths of my bucket handbag. I pulled it out and answered.

"Madison, it's John Sweet. I was hoping you'd answer. You aren't in the neighborhood, are you?"

"I'm at the pajama factory. Why? Is there a problem?"

"No, no problem. I forgot to mention yesterday that I'm working on a small memorial service for Alice—mostly family—out at Greenwood Cemetery and I'd love for you to come."

I wrestled with emotions in flux. Alice had told me her family wasn't close. On one hand, I knew the family would have their own memories to sort through and process. Even if their relationship with Alice was strained—or maybe because of that—they might not want outsiders present. John hadn't known of my existence and friendship with Alice until she left me the factory, and like most pitches from left field, that one must have come as a surprise. On the other hand, he was making an effort to include me, and that meant something.

"When is it?" I asked.

"I'm still working out the details, but it's going to be in the next day or so. Do any days work better than others for you?"

"Go ahead with your plans on your timetable. I'll make it work with mine."

"It's just—this might sound strange, but I was hoping you could help with things. Hire a caterer, plan the service, or design the programs. She'll need a tombstone too."

John's last-minute invitation for me to attend the as-yet unscheduled memorial service was feeling less and less generous. What he was asking of me was for him, not for Alice. I resented the manipulation.

When I didn't speak, John cleared his throat and then continued. "Or I'll have a funeral director plan something. She set aside some money to cover expenses."

"I think that's best." I changed the subject, pushing aside my personal opinions and focusing on business. "Regarding the factory, who would I need to contact to get inside?"

"What's the rush? That building hasn't gone anywhere for decades. I doubt it'll change now. Or are you hoping to sell it fast and make a profit?"

I bristled at his critical tone. "Before I make any firm decisions, I would like to see the interior. Yesterday you mentioned special-interest groups that lobbied to get the building unsealed. How would someone go about that?"

"I thought you understood how these things work. I'm filing the paperwork now, but you won't be able to take ownership for a couple of months. Plus, the building's been closed for a long time, and who knows what you'll find in there. I have that list of companies interested in the building if you want some leads. I could arrange something early next week if you want, maybe dig up a key and let you in myself. But right now, I have other things on my plate."

I couldn't explain the feeling that washed over me. Twenty-four hours ago, I hadn't even known about the factory, but for the moment, it felt like my own personal secret. Attending Alice's memorial would require socializing with a family who resented my inheritance, and from the sounds of John's voice, resented the inconvenience of Alice's death. But standing here, staring at the building in front of me, I felt a connection to my friend. I wanted to feel our friendship again without the judgment of strangers.

"If you don't mind, I'd rather discover the factory on my own. After I've been through it, if you'd like, I'd be happy to have you come out and see it for yourself."

He cleared his throat. "Like I told you, one of the lingering questions about the place is whether or not there's evidence inside that would shed light on the death of that pajama model. Your best bet is to contact the local police, introduce yourself, and have them unseal the place. But fair warning, some stones are better left unturned." He paused, and then added, "Let me know what you decide."

"Will do. Thanks, John. And thank you for letting me know about the memorial."

I hung up and stared at the building. John had told me to call the local police and introduce myself. Lucky for me, that introduction wasn't necessary. We'd been on a first-name basis for the past few years. I scrolled through the contacts on my phone and cued up the direct line to the new police captain.

"Captain Allen," Tex's familiar voice said.

"It's Madison."

"Hey, Night," he said. Maybe it was more accurate to say we were on a last-name basis. "Is this a friendly call or an I'm-in-trouble call?"

"I don't only call you when I'm in trouble," I said.

"Let's not argue the point. What's up?"

"I, um, have something I need to talk to you about. But it's not trouble. Well, maybe it is, but not the kind you're used to."

I could picture Tex at his desk, leaning back in his chair, running through the various times I'd had the kind of trouble that involved the police. A preemptive streak of defensiveness ignited within me, and I girded myself for whatever comments he planned to toss my way.

His reaction surprised me. "Is this urgent or can it wait? I just got a call about a situation downtown."

"It can wait," I said. Rocky stretched out the length of his leash and sniffed a patch of Bluebonnets.

"You're sure you're not in trouble?"

"Go handle your situation and call me later." I hung up.

I tugged Rocky's leash and studied the building again. The structure occupied most of the length of the block, comprised of white stucco and the occasional smaller white aluminum trim not unusual for the time. Lower floor windows had been blacked out on the inside. On the second through fourth floor, smaller windows occupied much of the façade, interrupted only by vertical brick columns that jutted out a few inches beyond the exterior. These windows were covered in grime that had built up over the decades while the factory sat abandoned. Toward the fourth floor, a few of the panes had been broken and covered by boards of wood. Dallas weather came with the occasional hail storm and heavy winds, and I wondered who had been responsible for the temporary fix that kept the interior safe from the elements.

I could picture a steady stream of young women out to get jobs for the first time coming to Sweet Dreams in the hopes of making enough of an income to take care of their families while their husbands and fathers were fighting. I'd like to have Clara here, I thought. Once I had a chance to get inside and air the place out, I'd like to invite her to give me a tour and hear her stories about what it was like all those many years ago. I wondered if enough time had passed for her to leave behind the memories of what had happened, or if they'd rise back to the surface once she was inside.

It was an odd thought. I'd left the town where I grew up so I wouldn't have to face my own painful memories ever again, yet so much of my life was about preserving the memories of others. I brushed the confusing thought aside and approached the front doors.

The main doors to the building were locked and doubly secured by a length of chain that wrapped around the handles. At first, it seemed like a poor attempt at security, until I tried to move the chain and realized how heavy it was.

I'd been so absorbed in my inspection of the exterior of the building that I hadn't noticed a small crowd of people approaching me. When they entered my field of vision, I jumped. There were five of them, men and women in ages ranging from late twenties to early forties I'd guess, though my determination was based on the fact that they all looked younger than I was. Two of the women held large white sheets of poster board, and a man toward the back held a two-by-four beam of wood in each of his hands. It was the man in the front who addressed me.

"Hey, lady!" he called out. "I'm Sid Krumholtz. I organized the rally. Did you bring your own sign?"

My confusion must have shown in my narrowed eyes and drawn brows. "What rally?" I asked. "What sign?"

"We're lobbying to get this building unsealed."

"Why?"

"It's been locked up for years, and now that the owner died we're going to demonstrate until the police get back in there and search for evidence."

Off in the distance, I heard a siren. It wasn't an unusual sound, but as it grew closer, I saw the inevitable direction things were headed. The man in front of the group thrust a picket sign at me. "Hold it up high so they can see it," he said. "Now you're one of us."

Two police cars and a Jeep pulled into the parking lot in front of the building. Uniformed officers got out of the cars. Tex got out of the Jeep. Even with his mirrored aviator shades on over his eyes, I could feel him glaring at me.

Great. Even though I'd done nothing wrong, thanks to a random series of events, I'd somehow ended up at the heart of Tex's "situation."

FIVE

Captain Tex Allen would have been an imposing figure striding across the lot toward me if we hadn't already sorted through most of his testosterone-fueled tendencies in the past. He'd joined the Lakewood PD when he was twenty-five and had worked his way up from officer to detective to lieutenant. His recent promotion to captain had been a surprise to a lot of people, less so to me when I considered what he'd lived through before his own captain had retired. He'd seized the opportunity for a promotion and a desk job. Our relationship had far more layers than I ever would have imagined and I'd come to view him as a friend. On the surface, he was an egotistical, arrogant, flirtatious womanizer, a.k.a. the opposite of everything I liked. I couldn't explain why I wanted him in my life, but I did. I guess when people show you what they hide below the surface, sometimes they surprise you.

The last time I saw Tex was six months ago. Our unexpected friendship seemed to flourish when I was in Palm Springs recently and turned to him to help me out with a situation involving their local police. I'd been vacationing with my handyman-turned-boyfriend Hudson James at the time, but his family had been at the center of the drama, and I'd needed an outside opinion. Tex had lent an unbiased ear, and I'd confided more to him than I'd planned. The physical distance between us had provided a buffer zone. You couldn't get much more outside than fourteen hundred miles away. Well, you could, but let's not quibble details.

Tex's recent promotion seemed to agree with him. He looked confident but not cocky. Relaxed but in control. Something about him had changed. In the past, I'd felt like he wanted to add me to the conquest column in his little black book. Today, not so much.

I shoved the picket sign back at Sid. "I'll be right back," I said. I walked toward Tex. Rocky ran ahead and wound his leash around Tex's legs. A commotion broke out behind me and I tried using non-verbal communication through eye rolling to let Tex know I had not planned to be a part of the rally.

"What's going on here, Night?" Tex asked.

"I'm not sure. I was just walking around, minding my business—"

Sid jogged to keep up with me and then elbowed me out of the way and stood in front of Tex. He glanced my way and then turned back to Tex. "I'm with the Truthers."

"Truthers?" I asked.

"We sleuth for the truth," he explained to me and then turned back to Tex. "This building may hold evidence that would reclassify the death of Suzy Bixby as a homicide and help catch her killer. We demand that you unseal the building and reopen the case. The owner died, and that makes the building public property."

"That's not true," I said.

Sid turned to me. He looked annoyed at my second interjection into the conversation, or maybe it was the fact that I'd told him he was wrong. "I'm the leader," he said. "I'm in charge."

"But you're wrong," I said. "I mean, you're right, the owner did pass away, but she willed the building to someone else, so you're wrong about it being public property."

Tex crossed his arms and tipped his head. The corners of

his mouth turned down. I was fairly sure Sid couldn't see me, so I crossed my eyes again and then looked out the corners of them at Sid in a series of expressions I'd seen Doris Day do hundreds of times over the course of her TV show. There was a very good chance Tex was not as fluent in Doris Day facial expressions as I was and he'd simply think I was having some sort of a seizure.

Tex pointed to Sid. "You, wait over there. I need to talk to this woman for a moment."

Sid, who moments ago had empowered me with a picket sign, now looked at me warily. He didn't have a clue what role I played at his demonstration, if any. He scanned my orange and white three-quarter-sleeved ensemble and my lime green sneakers and then looked at Rocky, who had succeeded in wrapping most of his leash around Captain Allen's suit pants. Sid seemed to decide I was not an immediate threat to whatever picketing efforts he'd coordinated. "I'll wait over here," he said, as if it were his idea and not Tex's instruction.

Tex said something to the uniformed officers, and they moved away from us with Sid. Tex looked down at Rocky, who stood up on his hind legs and put his paws on Tex's knee. Tex might be immune to my charms, but nobody could resist the sweet, joyful face of a Shih Tzu. Nobody.

After a few seconds, Tex bent down and ruffled Rocky's fur. I handed Tex the end of the leash, and he unwound it from around his legs and then handed it back to me. "What did I tell you when you called?"

"You said you had a situation and you would call me later."

"Nothing about that sentence would have told you where I was going. Do I want to know how you ended up involved with this group?"

"I didn't know you were coming here. You said you had a situation. For all I know, that meant the Lakewood PD coffee machine ran out of powdered creamer. I was standing on the sidewalk out front when I called you. I could just as easily accuse you of stalking me."

"How would I know you were here?"

"That's exactly my point. Can we move on?"

"What are you doing here, Night? Highlights only."

"Highlights: Alice Sweet, one of the nice old ladies who swims with me every morning, passed away. This building was her husband's pajama factory. She left it to me."

Tex's response would not have gained him favor among Christians. "Do you know the history of this building?"

"A little. That's why I called you. The lawyer said probate would likely take months and the only way I could get inside early would be to contact the police and arrange for it to be unsealed."

Tex dropped his head into his hands and buried his long fingers into the roots of his dark blond hair. When he looked up at me, he pulled off his aviators so I could see the stress in his clear blue eyes. "Do you know what kind of trouble you're going to cause?"

"I have an idea."

"And you can't wait."

"Whether I wait a few months or I get in now, there's going to be a big fuss. From what I've heard, Suzy Bixby's death happened two police captains ago. Captain Washington would have inherited the problem, and he left it in your lap when he retired. Ignoring it won't make it go away. Your department is in need of a pro-community publicity project, and you could get a lot of buzz out of this, if you wanted. Come on, don't you want to have a press conference so you can show off all those new suits you bought when you became captain? We could help each other."

"What's in it for you?"

"Maybe I'm one of them," I said. I pointed over my

shoulder to Sid and his crowd.

"I don't believe for a second you're one of them," he said. He looked over my head at the small group of picketers. I turned. A woman knelt on the sidewalk, correcting a spelling error on her sign. Sid spoke to the uniformed officers, who showed little interest in the conversation. The others stood to the left of the entrance in a casual huddle under a cloud of cigarette smoke.

"Fine," I said. "Ignore them and listen to me for a second. It wouldn't be the first time you had a chance to lay rest to old rumors. I know you know how powerful it is to get closure."

"We're not done talking about this," he said.

"I know we're not. I'm the one who called you first, remember?"

"You're going to be the death of me, Night. I can feel it. I'll handle this. Now go to your studio and paint something yellow."

Rush-hour traffic had died down, and I made it from Deep Ellum to Lakewood in under fifteen minutes. I parked behind my small studio in one of the three spaces in the lot and led Rocky inside.

As soon as his leash was unclipped, he took off for the front window. I watched him pace back and forth a few times, and then I retreated to my office.

February was a funny month for a decorator. Most people focused on their homes after the holidays, and my calendar had been booked solid in January. Things had trickled off in the past few weeks.

Because of that, I'd offered to coordinate the annual conclave of historic theater owners. Previous conclaves had been inspired by classic movies that we showed at The Mummy, the old-yet-still-operable theater where I volunteered. There'd been a tradition of musicals being at the heart of the fundraisers. *Guys and Dolls* had been a popular one, as had *West Side Story*.

This year, I'd proposed an outdoor picnic then a private cocktail party, capped with a midnight viewing of *The Pajama Game*. Richard Goode, the managing director of the theater, had begrudgingly accepted my proposal when no others had been submitted, despite his tastes leaning toward Italian Giallos and seventies noirs like *Taxi Driver*.

I pulled up my emails and saw a long list from Richard, one with the subject line WHO'S IN CHARGE OVER THERE? which made me wonder what he'd possibly found to include in the two he'd sent after that.

Dealing with Richard usually required a large dose of caffeine, so I cleaned out my vintage electric coffee pot, measured enough coffee grinds to get me through the day, and plugged the pot into an outlet. A spark shot out of the wall, and I threw my hands up in the air and jumped back. That was the problem with old appliances. As much as I loved my coffeepot, it seemed it was not long for this world.

I turned around and left the studio with my keys in my fist. I could handle the rest of the world changing underneath me, but Mad for Mod was special, and part of what made it special was how I surrounded myself with the items I loved.

Sure, an electric coffee pot was impractical compared to a Keurig or a trip to Starbucks. And the yellow donut phone was inconvenient when I needed a hands-free option while on a business call. But those were my choices. That was my business. Clients hired me because they knew I understood every single touch down to the smallest dingbat detail.

I unlocked the storage shed behind my studio and rooted amongst a loosely organized pile of Danish Modern furniture and atomic kitchen appliances until I found a backup electric coffee pot. The one in use was white with blue flowers; this one was clear glass with gold starbursts. The model was Corningware Starflite. I'd bought it for two dollars at Canton First Trade Days two years ago and had been keeping it in reserve for an emergency situation just like today.

I stood up straight and considered the rest of the items in my storage locker. There was easily ten times this much in an off-site location, plus the items that filled the detached garage of Thelma Johnson's house. Taking small jobs had moved a lamp here and a dresser there, but what was I waiting for? Maybe it was time to stop living a small life.

I returned to my office and brewed a new pot of coffee and then called Richard.

"It's about time you called me back. Didn't you get my emails?"

"Richard, you have me on the phone for the next ten minutes, and I haven't had any coffee yet today. What seems to be the problem?"

"The problem is I have fifty general managers of restored theaters coming to Dallas this weekend. Your assistant said she was sending an update two days ago and I've received nothing."

"She's not my assistant; she's my part-time employee. And you can't blame this on Connie. I was in the process of confirming everything yesterday when I found out a friend died."

"Yes, that happens when your friends are in their eighties."

"That was uncalled for."

"I know. I'm sorry. I'm just stressed out. Who died?"

"Alice Sweet. She's one of the ladies I met through morning swims."

"I read about her in the paper. Wasn't she married to the guy who owned Sweet Dreams Pajama Factory? That's great. We can change everything and have the picnic there."

"No, Richard. I can't get access to the building."

"Just contact the Historical Preservation Society of Dallas. They specialize in stuff like this. They'll get us in no problem."

"Richard, we don't need the Historical Preservation Society. I own the building. Alice left it to me."

"Great!"

"Not great. Richard, listen to me. I already lined up a picnic at the arboretum and a midnight showing of *The Pajama Game*. That's enough."

"Terrible film. The London revival wasn't bad, but it was no *Rent*. Besides, the Arboretum called and said they accidentally double booked our event and did we mind sharing the gardens with a twelve-year-old's birthday party?"

"And you said..."

"I said yes we minded. Turns out the twelve-year-old's parents have a lot more money than we do and we're out." He sighed. "You need to pull out all the stops on this one, Madison. These people know who you are. The only reason the national organization gave the conclave to us and not Houston is because they found out you volunteer here."

"Why would that make a difference?"

Richard groaned. "Because apparently your boyfriend is out in Hollywood making some kind of deal with his life story and that life story includes our theater."

"He *was* talking about a deal, but it fell through."

Last year, a husband-and-wife movie-production team had expressed interest in optioning Hudson's life story for a film. Shortly after their initial interest, the phone calls stopped and the interest dried up.

I hadn't voiced how I felt about the possibility of our lives being fodder for a film because it was Hudson's story that had been pursued, not mine. The situation affected several different people, but him the most, and I recognized that this might be a way for him to close that door to his past—the accusations and the judgment—for good. It turned out it was not to be.

"Already? You were supposed to be our meal ticket. You better act fast before the organization finds out you're yesterday's news. And I mean you, not your assistant. Since when are you doing so well you can afford to hire a staff? Maybe you should become a donor."

"I'm hanging up now."

I'd been surprised by Richard knowing about the pajama factory, but I shouldn't have been. He'd learned the same way I had: Alice's obituary. And while I'd only moved to Dallas in my mid-forties, Richard had grown up here. Between the local news and the internet, most people probably knew more about Sweet Dreams than I did. It was the way of the world.

I stared at my notes. Fifty general managers of restored theaters around the country were coming to Dallas to see The Mummy firsthand. They were due to arrive Friday morning. For the past month, Richard had been particularly stressed over the fact that his audience would be his peers, and thus his critics.

I wasn't a Luddite, but I'd always found a greater sense of creative thought with paper and pen vs. a computer. I grabbed a notebook and marker and carried them out to the showroom. Rocky sat in the front window with his nose pressed up against the glass.

"You miss Hudson's cat, don't you?" I said to him. "I guess sometimes you get lonely too." I ruffled his fur and then started making new plans for the theater manager event.

Just as I was jotting down the last of my notes, Rocky jumped up and stood on his hind legs with his paws on the window. A small tan and white Chihuahua stood on the sidewalk in front of him. Both of their tails wagged with enthusiasm. It was close to ten, our regular hours, so I set my notebook down and stood up, and then unlocked the front door.

The small dog appeared nervous and walked backward a

few steps, and then turned around and trotted away from me. Rocky, who had never once tried to leave the studio when someone opened the door, nuzzled my ankle and pushed his nose through the opening and then took off down the street after the unfamiliar dog.

SIX

"Rocky!" I said. I ran out the front door after him. The Chihuahua was at the far corner of the block. Rocky yipped and the Chihuahua took two steps toward us, barked several times, and then, when then the sound of a car engine approached, turned around and ran away. Rocky ran after him, but the small dog disappeared around the corner. I caught up to Rocky and carried him back to Mad for Mod. We were both slightly dejected.

As much as I wanted to leave work and get to Hernando's Hide-It-Away, it was bad business for me to close the studio in the middle of the day. I spent the better part of the next two hours sketching out an idea for the front-window display while waiting for my friend and part-time employee, Connie Duncan, to arrive for her shift.

After years of job loyalty to a car-insurance company, she'd been laid off last month. While she conducted the sort of self-analysis that one does when faced with an outdated resume, I gave her part-time hours to pad her work experience and allow me to keep the studio open while I was out in the field. Connie's dream was to go into business for herself like me, but she had yet to latch onto an idea with legs.

Connie was half of a hipster couple whose kitchen I'd remodeled. Her husband, Ned, was a band promoter. He was out of town on a business trip, which always made Connie get a little rambunctious.

She arrived shortly after one. "Hey," she said, dumping her straw handbag on the floor. "What's cooking around here?"

I shrugged. "No appointments, if that's what you're asking."

She dropped into the chair in front of my desk. "I'm so bored. This morning I detailed the stove and tonight I'm planning on cleaning the grout in the kitchen with a cotton swab and some bleach. Ned is in Nashville, and I'm all alone. It's not fair, you know? I need a job that's going to let me travel to exotic places too."

I laughed. "Nashville is exotic?"

"It's better than Dallas. Nothing happens in Dallas." I raised an eyebrow. "Nothing happens to *me* in Dallas," she clarified.

"Be careful what you wish for."

She sat up and flipped through a catalog for ceramic tile and then closed it and tossed it onto my desk. "You have to come over tonight. Please. My house is cleaner than it's been in over a year. Or is Hudson coming back? Please don't say Hudson's coming home tonight. I mean, yes, you probably miss him and all, but for real, Mads, I'm crawling the walls. Last night I started an Etsy shop for one-of-a-kind jacket sleeves for old vinyl records."

"Is there a market for that?"

"How should I know? It seemed like a good idea at two thirty in the morning when I pulled out my Tom Jones album and noticed the original jacket was torn. Ask me in a week. But tonight? Girls' night? Please?"

"Hudson's still in California. That job is finally on schedule and now that he put some of his own money into it, he wants to see it through."

The vacation with Hudson in Palm Springs had been a working one. Hudson's brother-in-law had invested in some land and had plans to develop it into a one-of-a-kind strip mall using restored mid-century architectural details. I'd gone along to help with the design aspect. A murder and a drug ring kept the project from sticking to schedule, and by the time the anticipated two weeks were up, I was ready to come home. Hudson became an investor in the property and stayed in Palm Springs to help get the project back on track.

"Good! I'll call Joanie from the thrift store, and Babe from the paint store and Carol from the hardware store. We can get takeout and play Parcheesi. I just got a reprint of the original board game. It's gorgeous!"

"Maybe," I said. I chewed my lower lip. "Remember I got that call yesterday about an inheritance?"

"Yes. What was it? Anything interesting or the usual?"

"Definitely not the usual."

I told Connie about Sweet Dreams but kept quiet about the letter and the storage unit. Until I knew what Alice had left for me, I didn't want to get my hopes up about the factory or the possibilities of what I could do with it.

If the interior was in as much disarray as the exterior, there might not be anything worth salvaging inside the building. Sid and his protesters could picket all they wanted, but if the critters of Dallas had been occupying the interior, there was a pretty solid chance anything related to a crime had long since been eaten and pooped out. I'd yet to hear of anyone extracting clues from a rat turd. Forensic scientists were good, but they weren't *that* good.

I left Rocky with Connie and drove the short distance from Mad for Mod to Hernando's on Mockingbird Lane. Although the east/west street had become heavily trafficked by those trying to avoid highways, I usually enjoyed my time sitting in traffic because most of the houses in this neighborhood were from the fifties and sixties. My favorites were three houses on Shook Avenue designed by Arch Swank. They each had the appearance of ranch houses on stilts. The bottom story was the garage. Swank was more known for having designed two of the local Neiman Marcus locations, but his houses had a charm about them that always made me smile.

Yet today, even driving past those classic red brick and white trim residences, I couldn't shake the uneasy, nervous feeling that something about my life had changed and I was trying too hard to keep it the same. I was distracted in a way I rarely experienced, and with a mounting list of projects tugging at my time, I felt anxious.

Hernando's Hide-It-Away was easily visible from a few blocks away. Built in the same style as many of the nondescript, budget-friendly hotels in the area, the storage units were white brick, clay roof, and occasional external detail in the rough stone that had become popular in the nineties. The logo stood out in colorful neon tubing mounted on black above a faded print-shop banner that simply said, "Your Neighborhood Storage Solutions." I wondered what kind of business people had thought this was to inspire the addition of the banner.

I parked my Alfa Romeo in a space by the front door and went inside. Empty boxes and bubble wrap were set out in stacks around the shopfront.

A young woman, probably in her twenties, was behind the counter. She was dressed in a black pantsuit that was a little snug, as if she'd gained five pounds and the fabric didn't accommodate the weight. She had straight brown hair that hung just past her shoulders, bangs that were swept to the side, and a fresh-faced innocence that came with not yet having experienced her first major life tragedy. A white plastic tag with the name "Rachel" was pinned on her lapel.

"Good morning!" she said brightly. "Is it still morning? No? But it's not afternoon. What is it? Noon? But nobody says 'good noon.' Why not? We should start a trend. Good noon!" She smiled.

"Good noon to you too," I said and returned her smile. "I'm here about a storage unit."

"Okay, yes. We have those. Do you know what size you want? I can get prices for you."

"I already have one." I held up my key. "I just don't know where it is."

"Oh! That's different." She reached forward and checked the tag on the key. "One eighty-five. Come with me."

I followed Rachel outside the office to a small open golf cart. The soles of her mid-heeled shoes made a clicking sound against the gravel. I trailed behind her, silent in my sneakers. I'd given up fancy shoes a long time ago after my knee injury and hadn't looked back since.

I'd assumed from the golf cart that the storage locker wasn't within walking distance, but Rachel rounded the corner and parked by the building behind the main office. I followed her through a set of double doors and into an elevator big enough to hold a couple of flatbed hand trolleys.

When the doors opened on the second floor, she exited and turned right. She spun a dial mounted on the wall, and flickering lights turned on overhead. She pointed past me. "Yours is about halfway down the hall on the right-hand side."

Until she left me alone to test out the key in the padlock, I hadn't truly believed this would work. But the key turned, and the padlock snapped open. I waited until the sound of Rachel's small golf-cart engine started up and drove back around to the front of the building before swinging the door open and switching on the lamp inside.

Alice's storage unit was empty except for a square metal box that sat on a small wooden stool inside. The box lid was hinged on one side, and the top was in place. When I opened the box lid and flipped it back, I gasped.

Alice had hinted about the history of the pajama factory and had told me about the accumulation of clippings she'd left for me to find.

She hadn't said anything about leaving me a gun.

SEVEN

A small black pistol rested on top of a carefully folded pile of yellowed newspaper articles. There was no reason for me to fear picking it up, but I did. I didn't particularly like guns, and finding one in a storage unit that I'd been sent to by a woman who couldn't explain her actions was beyond the scope of what I could process. I shut the box and kept my hand on top of it like it held a live snake that wanted to get out. Leaving me a gun didn't feel like something Alice would do.

Something wasn't adding up.

After a few seconds, I reopened the box and took a picture of the gun with my phone. Without disturbing the contents, I closed the box. I locked the storage unit and left the building. The gun was one more thing for me to add to the list to tell Tex. No point waiting for his call now. This bore more than a passing resemblance to a police matter.

I walked out front and climbed into my car, but instead of starting the engine, I pulled out my phone. Wherever he was, he'd have his cell.

"Allen," he answered.

"It's Madison."

"Where are you? I came by your studio, and that kooky woman was there. She said it was a last-minute arrangement. You weren't painting a picket sign, were you?"

"I'm at a storage facility on the corner of Mockingbird and Alderson Street. The woman who left me the pajama factory left me a key to a unit and I came here to find out what was inside. I found a gun. I think maybe, possibly, what started out as a one-person project for me is quickly going to turn into a two-person collaboration."

"Between you and me."

"Yes."

"Where are you now? Exact location."

"I'm in my car in front of the rental-unit office to Hernando's Hide-It-Away, in the parking space next to the handicap space that faces the front door. I'm about two inches closer to the left side of my space than the right. Is that exact enough for you?"

"Wait there. I'm on my way."

Tex's Jeep parked next to me a few minutes later. The sun had gotten hot, and I'd moved my car to the shade of a tree on the property. Still, it's not hard to spot a vintage blue Alfa Romeo in a parking lot that had eight spaces and no other customers.

Tex parked alongside me. He climbed out of his Jeep and tipped his head toward the building. "Show me what you saw."

Before Tex's promotion, he was a polo-shirt-and-jeans guy. These days, the job called for a suit and tie. I would have figured him to be uncomfortable, but he appeared to take it in stride. He reached the doors slightly before me and went in first. I followed.

Rachel, the employee who had walked me to the storage unit when I'd arrived the first time, was back in her position behind the counter. Before she could launch into the pros and cons of a noon greeting, I reintroduced myself and told her Tex was helping me with the storage locker. She studied him for a few seconds too long but seemed to approve of what she saw, giving him a coy smile. He winked at her. I shook my head at the display and then led him through the side door to the back building.

Minutes later, Tex and I were standing in front of the unlocked storage unit staring at the gun. It was exactly where I'd left it, nestled on top of a pile of newspaper clippings.

"That is a gun," he said. "You don't know anything about it? Your friend didn't tell you it was here or why she locked it up?"

"She never mentioned she owned a gun. She never mentioned the storage unit or the factory, either, so I'm going to go out on a limb here and say Alice had some secrets."

Tex stared at the weapon for a few more seconds. "If you're worried about the gun, I can tell you a few things that might help. This is a Glock 9mm. It's the most popular gun on the market. I'll want to have it tested by our forensics guys, but it appears to be in good condition. It couldn't have been involved in the death of Suzy Bixby—or anybody else who died when the pajama factory was in business—because it hadn't even been produced yet."

"You can tell all that from looking at it?"

He shrugged. "Kind of like you looking at numbers on the front of a building and knowing who the architect was."

"Richard Neutra."

"Whoever."

"No, Neutra is the one who designed his own numbers."

He grinned. He picked up the gun and looked underneath. "Do you know what the rest is?" he asked, indicating the contents.

"I think they're newspaper clippings about the factory, but I didn't have a chance to look at them."

He picked up the folder and handed it to me. For the second time that day I closed and locked the door to the storage unit. We left. Rachel watched us walk to our separate cars. She smiled broadly, but this time her attention was on Tex. I glanced at him. He smiled at her, and a light blush crept up her cheeks.

Rachel's eyes darted to me.

Tex slowed down. I didn't. I reached my car first. When I turned around, I saw him lingering by the office. "I should be getting back to the studio," I said. "Are we good here?"

"Give me a minute," he said.

I looked at Tex and then at Rachel. I wasn't certain, but it looked like she'd undone one of the buttons on her blouse to expose more cleavage. I looked back at Tex. "One minute," I said, holding up my index finger.

Tex followed Rachel inside. I sat in my car under the shade of the tree. As much as I wanted to dig into the newspaper clippings, I wanted to sort them out in an organized manner and not risk damaging them or getting them out of order. Starting the process in the open front seat of a convertible while a breeze ruffled the branches of the tree over my head probably wasn't a good idea.

About a minute later, Tex came out of the office. He crossed the lot and leaned down on my car, resting his forearms on the passenger-side door.

"Everything okay?" I asked. "The employee looked at us funny. You don't think she saw the gun in your pocket, do you?"

He laughed. "That's not why she looked at us that way."

"What's your theory?"

"You were here by yourself, and then you came back with me. She thinks we were fooling around in the storage locker."

I rolled my eyes. "You have a one-track mind," I said.

At that moment, the doors opened, and Rachel ran out. She scanned the parking lot and smiled when she saw Tex. "Captain Allen," she called out and waved.

"Hold that thought," Tex said. He stood straight and walked away from me. I readjusted my seat in the car so I could get a better view.

I'd never been the kind of woman who knew how to flirt, so

watching this was like having a front-row seat at a training demonstration. Even without being close enough to hear, I could tell exactly what Rachel wanted, and it had nothing to do with Tex's potential as a storage-rental customer.

Two hair flips, one seductive smile, and a brief moment where she touched her hand to her clavicle, and I was done. Tex knew where to find me if he needed me. I started my car, threw it into gear, and whipped it in a reverse semicircle out of my space and the parking lot.

I drove to Mad for Mod and parked behind the studio. My small lot only had three parking spaces and two were occupied: one with Connie's car and one with an unfamiliar one. I parked in the third and let myself in through the back door. I poked my head into the closed office. Rocky was on his bed, chewing on his rope bone. Two female voices were arguing in the front of the studio. I eased the door shut before Rocky could come out and followed the argument.

"I have to talk to the owner," said the customer.

"The owner will be back this afternoon. You can talk to her then," Connie said.

"I'm not going anywhere. I'm not leaving until I talk to Madison Night," the other voice insisted.

From my position in the hallway, I could see Connie and the customer, but they appeared to not yet know I was there. I stayed behind the wall but leaned forward to size up the woman who seemed so interested in talking to me.

So often, it was easy to identify potential clients of a mid-century modern decorating business. Sometimes it was a vintage handbag or a late sixties color palette. Sometimes it was a hairstyle, or a copy of *Atomic Ranch* magazine in their hand, or even an Elvis ringtone on their cell phone. But the woman arguing with Connie had none of those tells. In fact, in her fitted black suit and high red patent-leather heels, she was the antithesis of everything I and my decorating business stood for, which made me all the warier about her presence. Still, I was the boss for a reason.

I came out from behind the wall. "Connie, I'm back," I said brightly. "Hello," I said to the woman. "I'm Madison Night, owner of Mad for Mod." I held out my hand.

"I know exactly who you are," she said. She raised her finger and jabbed at the air in front of me. "I don't want to hear about you sticking your nose where it doesn't belong. Stay away from my investigation, or you'll be sorry." She whirled around and stormed out the door.

EIGHT

I looked at Connie. "Who was that?"

She held up a finger. "Give it a second."

The doors to my studio reopened, and the woman walked back in. A shot of adrenaline coursed through me and I braced myself for a confrontation. This time, the woman's body language was completely different. She was relaxed and appeared happy. I didn't know what kind of nut job I was dealing with, but I wished I'd had the foresight to ask Tex to meet me back here.

The woman threw one hand up in the air and said, "Ta-da! How was that?"

"How was what?"

"My audition. I mean, I know you aren't the one who makes the decisions, but you've got to have some say in the matter. After all, it was your life too."

I looked from her to Connie and back. "I'm a little lost."

"You don't know who I am?" the woman said. She was surprised. "You mean you really believed I was mad at you? That's the best possible reaction. Wait until I tell my agent!"

"Your agent? Are you...you are..."

"I'm an actress! And you have just Made. My. Day. I'm Erin Haney."

I held out my hand awkwardly. "I'm Madison Night."

"I know. I'd know you anywhere." She pushed my hand aside. "I'm a hugger!" she exclaimed and threw her arms around me.

When she let go, I took a step back. Connie looked at Erin and applauded. "Great job. You even had me going, and you told me what you were going to do."

I put both hands up. "Will one of you please tell me what's going on? I'm officially lost. Did we have an appointment? Am I supposed to know why you were just yelling at me?"

Erin giggled. "I'm an actress. Well, mostly, I'm a dancer, but I want to be an actress. My agent told me about a movie being made about some guy from Dallas, so I came here to check things out. Nobody knows I'm here, either. It's a research trip so I can get into the mindset of the character. Like method acting, you know?"

"You're talking about what happened to Hudson," I said slowly. Before my relationship with Hudson had turned toward romance, he'd been my handyman. And before that, he'd lived a quiet life, avoiding town gossip about a twenty-year-old unsolved murder case where he'd been a person of interest. A few years ago, the killer had resurfaced, and Hudson's reputation had been shattered. The evidence that connected him to the crime became front-page news. It was then that he dropped his protective walls and I saw the vulnerability he'd kept hidden while we worked together. After that harrowing time in our lives was over, my own emotional walls were left full of cracks.

"You're his girlfriend, right?" Erin asked.

"Yes, but you do know I have no say in the movie casting," I said. "To be honest, I thought the project had been abandoned."

Erin looked unfazed. "That's how the business works. People talk and ideas move from one company to another until someone decides to take a chance. My agent had coffee with a reporter from *Variety* who used to date a story scout for the original studio. Casting will take place in Los Angeles with the producer and directors, but I was hoping to spend some time with you while I'm here, pick up some pointers, maybe try out a few scenes. You know better than almost anybody what happened."

That was true, but it didn't mean I wanted to reenact it. I glanced back down at Erin's outfit. "You do know the killer targeted women dressed like Doris Day, right? Do you even know who Doris Day is?"

"Of course, I know who Doris Day is. She's the mayor of Carmel, California."

"That's Clint Eastwood. But she does live there, so points for that."

"Oh, wait. She was in a Hitchcock movie, and she likes animals, doesn't she?"

"Yes. She runs an animal foundation."

"Called Shambala Preserve, right?"

"No, that's Tippi Hedren."

"Okay. Hold on, I know this. She's the one who everybody thought was two years younger than she actually is, right? There was a big scandal when MSN dug up her birth certificate right before her ninety-fifth birthday."

"I'm not sure how big of a scandal it was, but yes, that was her. You know, that whole case Hudson and I were involved in had to do with one of her most famous movies, *Pillow Talk*. Maybe you should watch it?"

She waved her hands back and forth in front of her like a toddler who's being forced to eat peas. "I don't want anything to cloud my vision," she said. "Besides, I'm not going for one of the Doris Day parts. I figure there were so many women who looked the same that nobody's going to remember any of those actresses."

Considering most days I stuck out like the oddball of Dallas, it was somewhat comforting to be thought of as interchangeable for once. "Who do you want to play?" I asked politely.

"Officer Nasty!" she said.

As if the situation couldn't get any worse.

If a mid-century modern interior decorator who modeled her life after Doris Day could have a nemesis, I imagined none better than Officer Donna Nast. I'd resisted using the nickname her fellow officers used behind her back until I'd gotten to know her and discovered the nickname fit. You wouldn't think we'd have many reasons to spend time together, but somehow, she kept turning up in my life.

"Officer Nast played a very minor role in that case."

"Yes, but this is Hollywood. I heard they're going to write a steamy love scene between her and the police lieutenant." She waggled her eyebrows at that prospect.

"I guess if someone buys the story, they can take as many licenses with the truth as they want."

She shrugged. "It's all about happily ever after. You ended up with Hudson, but the hot cop deserves somebody too."

Happily ever after. Right.

Erin and Connie remained out front discussing the highs and lows of living in Dallas. I excused myself and went to my office. As soon as the door was shut and locked behind me, I called Hudson.

"Hey, Lady," he said. "You caught me on a break. Everything okay?"

"You tell me. An actress just showed up and told me she wanted to rehearse scenes before her audition for your movie. Were you going to tell me about this?"

Hudson chuckled. "If there were something to tell, I would." His deep Johnny Cash baritone sounded entertained by my reaction.

"This was just a random coincidence? That she showed up at my studio pretending to be Officer Nasty?"

"Not entirely random, although I do question her choice of character. There's been some talk. A couple of calls. I thought about telling you, but I didn't want to drag you back into any of it until I knew if it was going to go anywhere or stall out like the last time this came up."

I looked at the situation from Hudson's perspective. "They're showing interest in your story, and you're out there thinking about how I'm going to react. That's not fair to you."

"I don't want to split hairs, but to be accurate, they're *not* showing interest in my story, at least not the people who approached me originally. This new studio is a whole other deal. It's a cable channel that leans toward mysteries with romances, and I suspect if they go for it, the result won't have much to do with reality."

"Does that bother you?"

"It is what it is. I'm just along for the ride. What's going on there?"

I settled into my Barcelona chair and rested my head on the back of it. "Do you remember Alice Sweet? My friend from the pool?"

"Sure."

"She passed away recently and left me a pajama factory."

"Sorry to hear that. She was a nice lady. But a pajama factory? That's a first, right?"

"Yes. I didn't even know she owned one."

"Any idea why she left it to you?"

The thing was, I still didn't. The letter and the gun made me think something had been going on in Alice's life, something she'd never spoken of. Maybe she wanted me to clear her husband's name of the rumors like I'd first thought, or maybe she just figured I'd enjoy the novelty of the building. Maybe I'd been correct that she felt leaving it to one of her estranged step-children would have been too much of a burden. If there had been a dying wish in that letter, I'd have some clear direction, and I'd honor it. But for now, I was juggling the acceptance of her death with what I'd learned about the factory and the death of Suzy Bixby. "Who knows with Alice?" I said. "She was an interesting woman. You lived here your whole life. You never heard any rumors about the building?"

"I never went in much for rumors," he said.

We chatted a few more minutes. A part of me wanted to tell him about the gun, but I didn't. I tried convincing myself it was because I didn't want to worry him. I wasn't sure I believed it.

When I returned to the showroom, Erin was gone. I highlighted my idea for a new display window to Connie. We worked side by side breaking down the current window, vacuuming the platform and dusting the baseboards and window frame. Rocky's ball chair got relegated to the back corner. I expected him to follow us and sit in its new location, but instead he remained by the front of the shop staring out at the street.

"What's out there, Rock? What could he possibly find so fascinating on Greenville Avenue?" I asked absentmindedly.

"He's probably watching for the Chihuahua that wanders around during the day. I, um, I started leaving out food, and now we've got some stray cats. The Chihuahua hasn't come back."

"He chased a Chihuahua down the street earlier." I ruffled Rocky's fur. "Is that it? You made a new friend?"

"I made a video. Look." She pulled out her phone and showed me a GIF she'd taken from the street of Rocky on his hind legs with his paws on the inside of the glass. "Pretty cute, right? I thought you could use it in your advertising. I could mock something up for you if you want. Maybe you can give me a recommendation, and I can build up a client base. You know, if the custom record sleeve business doesn't take off?"

"Or maybe I could give you full-time hours."

Connie's eyes got big. "Don't toy with me, Madison."

"I'm not. I've been thinking now that I sold off my apartment building, I have the time and the wherewithal to take on bigger projects. My only problem is I need to find those bigger projects, and I can only do so much from the studio. You've been great helping me out so far, but I don't like feeling like I'm taking advantage of you. What do you think?"

"I think I love you."

"Let's not get carried away."

The window turned out beautifully. We put a white Saarinen tulip table in the center of the display and positioned four tulip chairs around it. The cushions on the chairs had been destroyed over time, but Connie set up a sewing machine and whipped out four matching bark cloth covers with a retro space theme. I used my limited knowledge of electrical wiring to hang a Sputnik lamp over the table, and replaced a few of the small white bulbs with blue and green ones.

Next, we set each place setting with round silver placemats and, using a mix-and-match assortment of Franciscan atomic starburst and Taylorstone Cathay patterns, created whimsical place settings. While Connie cleaned and dried a glass vase to use as the centerpiece, I dug out a couple of boxes of small silver jacks that I'd picked up in Canton for twenty-five cents a bag. I spritzed them with a light coating of bright chrome spray paint, and when they were dry, transferred them to each of the place settings. I then set a small vintage rocket ship toy in blast-off position on each of the bread plates and finished with four tall Royal China glasses with colorful turquoise graphics. The resulting window was cheerful and spacey. My favorite combination.

The window display had achieved the necessary purpose of distracting me from thoughts of Alice's death, Hudson's and my life being turned into a movie, and the surprise "audition" for the part of Nasty. But by the end of the day, all I wanted was to lock up the studio and dig into the file I'd taken from the storage unit. Connie and I mapped out her schedule for the next two weeks, and I headed home.

Tex's Jeep was parallel-parked by the hedges that lined my property. I parked behind it. The neighborhood was quiet, so I picked up Rocky and carried him instead of putting his leash back on. When we got past the shrubs that provided privacy from the road, Rocky saw Tex sitting on the front steps. He wriggled around until I set him down and he charged over to his friend.

Tex bent down and ruffled Rocky's fur and then straightened up. "Where'd you take off to this morning?"

I adjusted my bag with the files. "It looked to me like you had a shift in priorities. I was giving you the space to make your move."

"Come on, Night, that's not how I operate. I was there with you on the job."

Rocky ran into the yard and dug up one of his stuffed toys. He carried the dirt-covered animal—this one a fish—to Tex and dropped it by Tex's feet. Tex picked it up and threw it back into the yard, and Rocky chased after it.

"After I left Hernando's, I thought you'd want to know I confirmed your gun wasn't used in any open investigations," Tex said.

"So we're good. Alice probably got it for safekeeping but changed her mind about shooting it. She was uncomfortable having it in the house."

"Well, there's one problem with that theory."

"What's that?"

"Ballistics reports indicate the gun was fired as recently as this past week."

NINE

"That's impossible," I said. "Alice died two days ago, and she made out her will before that. The idea of her firing a gun in her last week alive and then putting it in her storage unit doesn't sound like her."

I had my keys in my hand, and I unlocked the front door and led the procession of person-person-dog through the solarium into the kitchen. I dumped everything on the table and went directly to the refrigerator for two bottles of water. I cracked the cap on one and tossed it, and held the other bottle out toward Tex. He waved it off.

"Night, take your emotions out of this. You're assuming everything you know about your friend is true."

"I don't want to take my emotions out of this. Alice trusted me with something. Besides, I can't see how she did this. Her health was declining, but she clung to her routine. Even when she couldn't swim, she had one of the other ladies drive her to the pool so she could rest on the deck with her ankles in the water. Hiding a gun in the storage unit the week before she died is too out of character. She doesn't drive. How did she get there? Who helped her? It doesn't make sense."

"How did you first find out she passed away?"

"I read the obituaries like I do every day. I was thinking of calling the law firm to offer my assistance with her estate. Not to benefit from her passing, but to simply help. I had no idea about the inheritance or the pajama factory or anything until her grandson called me. He works for the law firm executing her estate."

"He's the one who told you about the storage unit?"

"No, he gave me a letter from Alice. It was sealed, and the key was in the envelope."

"Can I see it?"

I pulled the envelope out of my handbag and handed it to Tex. He pulled the sheets of paper out and scanned them. His cop face was on, but twice I saw something else flicker in his eyes. He stared at the paper longer than I thought it would have taken him to read it then finally set it down on my kitchen table. He looked directly at me but didn't say a word for an uncomfortable couple of seconds. I was trying to gauge what sort of response to expect.

"There's no need to worry about that gun. Technically it belongs to you. Since we have zero evidence that it was used in a crime, I have no reason to hold on to it."

"I'm in no hurry to use it. Why don't you consider it an indefinite loan? Do with it what you will."

"It wouldn't be the worst thing in the world for you to learn how to defend yourself. A lot of crazies out there."

"Guns kill people."

"People kill people."

"I don't think I'm going to change my mind on this," I said. And considering the oak tree in my backyard had a bullet wound courtesy of Tex, I didn't think he'd change his mind either.

We had a brief stare-off for another couple of seconds. I secretly declared victory when he dropped his gaze to the table and rapped his knuckles on it. "Tell you what. I'll nose around a bit, see if I can shake something loose. How about we meet up at the pajama factory tomorrow morning and check it out together?"

I looked at him suspiciously. "Why are you being so nice to

me?"

"Community service." He picked up an apple from the bowl on the table, tossed it in the air, and caught it easily. He pointed at me while holding the apple. "Wear one of those swirly cotton dresses. I miss those."

I pointed to the exit. He bit into the apple and then left.

I pulled a frozen Lean Cuisine out of the freezer and turned the oven on, and then sat down at the table to go through the file. I'd considered asking Tex to stick around and help me sort through the clippings but selfishly chose to keep that task for myself. Alice and I hadn't had the kind of friendship where we emailed or texted every day, but still, I felt her absence. Despite the theories Tex had floated, the gun didn't feel like the Alice I knew. I was hoping the newspaper articles would.

My dinner grew cold. I ate a couple of forkfuls, enough to stave off hunger, but found myself much more interested in the rumors surrounding Sweet Dreams Pajama Factory than in my Chicken Enchilada Suiza. Somewhere after eleven, my eyes had a hard time focusing on the newsprint in front of me. I'd long since gotten the highlights of what the media had said about Alice's husband's business, or more appropriately, the reason for its inevitable closure. It boiled down to a couple of irrefutable facts and a much larger assortment of hypotheses.

Sweet Dreams Pajama Company had been showing steady growth through the second half of the forties into the fifties. Expansion into print advertising that capitalized on the desire of women to be treated equally in the workforce tapped into the fifties zeitgeist.

Suzy Bixby had been hired to model the 1954 winter pajama collection. It was the first time Sweet Dreams had produced His and Hers pajamas out of matching fabric, and in the company's promotional campaign much had been made of Suzy's family's standing in Dallas and her desirability amongst local suitors.

With two older sisters, Suzy wasn't the first of the Bixbys to catch the eye of the media, but she was the only one to debut with the endorsement of the Idyllwild Club, a social organization that had maintained control over the debut process in Dallas since the late 1800s. Suzy's debut came after World War II had ended, and the attention lavished upon her matched the celebratory feel of the post-war era.

The oppression of the war years was history, and working girls were in their jobs as much to meet eligible bachelors as to support their families. Where a toughness had settled in on the shoulders of women like Suzy's older sister Clara, Suzy captured everything the young women of the fifties wanted to be: glamorous, desirable, and in charge.

Her unexpected death at twenty-one, therefore, cast a particularly unexpected shadow over the company that had initially supplied her limelight and subsequently, over the personal character of owner George Sweet. The twice-married father of two refused to comment on rumors of a relationship between himself and the deceased model, closing the company overnight and taking a job as a traveling salesman that kept him on the road for most of the year. Sweet Dreams, which initially gained a reputation for equal opportunity employment, left over a hundred employees without benefits overnight. Because of the unexpected move, any goodwill Sweet Dreams had garnered in the community had long since soured.

I tucked the newspaper clippings back into the folder and shrugged my shoulders in a backward circle to help work out the kinks I'd encouraged by hunching over the table for the past few hours. Article after article added to the rumors, but at the core of the legend, one thing existed: Suzy Bixby died after a steamer malfunctioned at Sweet Dreams Pajama Company. A burst of steam heat left her with severe burns. She was hospitalized and treated but died from complications less than twenty-four hours after the accident. Suzy's life had held much promise, and the court of public opinion wanted someone to blame. George was it.

The article did as much to ignite my curiosity as it did to satisfy it. Over the years, the accidental death of Suzy had become sensationalized to where it had become more local lore than tragedy. But as time passed, it went from being discussed on the anniversary of the accident to every five years, and only as a short item that filled an oddball amount of space in print media. Once newspapers shifted to online editions, the story of Suzy Bixby's death existed only on nostalgia websites that had hardly any followers. I wanted to talk to Clara and find out what it had been like in those days directly following the incident, yet I didn't know how to broach the subject without coming across as crass.

And while I knew Suzy was the victim in all of this, I couldn't help wondering what it had been like for Alice to live through. To first have a young model die in her husband's factory was bad enough, but to hear the rumors that he'd had something to do with her death was worse. And instead of denying it, he'd closed the doors to the company he'd built from scratch and chose a new career that kept him on the road where he couldn't answer questions.

I hadn't known George, but his actions did little to make me want to defend him.

The next morning, the alarm arrived unwelcome. In the fog of sleep, I hit the snooze button and rolled over. Fragmented bits of information that I'd read the previous night pierced the cloudy mental state I'd achieved through sleep, and I knew I wouldn't return to dreams. My muscles needed a workout, and my curiosity needed another conversation with Clara. I grabbed my swim bag, clipped on Rocky's leash, and headed for the Gaston Swim Club.

But Clara wasn't at the pool this morning. At ninety-four years old, she certainly had the prerogative to sleep in if she wanted. Still, I found myself more disappointed than understanding. I completed my morning workout, achieving only one of the two goals I'd set out to accomplish by showing up.

I dressed in a red and white windowpane sheath dress with a red leather belt that ended in two thick tassels. The dress had short sleeves and patch pockets. I pulled on red tights and matching Keds, ate a banana, and drank a bottle of orange juice that I'd packed from home. I picked Rocky up from the doggy day care and left to meet Tex at the pajama factory as arranged. The morning sunlight cast a radiant glow over the congested traffic on the highway. I quickly changed course and drove an intersecting path of side streets to avoid the segment of the population that was headed in to work, arriving at the pajama factory a few minutes after eight. Rocky led the way, keeping the leash taut as he ran ahead of me toward the building. I was surprised not only to see Tex already there but in conversation with a man I didn't know. The two men turned to face me as I approached.

I smiled politely at the stranger and then glared at Tex. We were going to have to establish some non-verbal communication soon. "Captain Allen, you didn't mention we'd have company on our walk-through."

"That's really up to you."

The man held out his hand. "Dax Fosse," he said. "Historical Preservation Society of Dallas."

"Madison Night." I shook his hand.

Dax was a young man with prematurely gray hair inconsistent with his youthful face and outfit of a vintage blazer over a concert T-shirt. He wore heavy black eyeglasses, an almost geeky style. The resulting effect was that he'd seen this look on a reporter from Rolling Stone magazine and had copied it to the letter.

"Hope you don't mind me crashing your party this morning." He glanced down at Rocky, who was sniffing the white rubber toe of his Converse sneaker.

"How did you know we would be here?" I asked.

"Richard Goode called us. He said you work for him."

"I work *with* him, not *for* him. Why would he call you?"

"He said you're planning an event for him and wanted me to help you get the permits so you could use the building."

"I don't want to use this building for anything—at least not anything that has to do with Richard's event. But I still don't understand what you have to do with it."

"How much do you know about Sweet Dreams?" Dax asked.

"A little."

"It's one of a couple of interesting buildings that the HPSD monitors around Dallas. A Google Alert popped up about the building changing hands. Took a couple of phone calls after that, but we found out what we needed to know."

I looked at Tex, confused. He shrugged as if it were no big deal. It was *definitely* a big deal.

"Which is what?" I asked. "What do you need to know?"

"Surely by now you understand the historical significance of the factory," Dax said. "Sweet Dreams was the first company in Dallas to employ more than fifty percent women. Half of the families in Dallas have roots in the city because the Sweets had the guts to train women to work the line."

"Yes," I said, "I had an idea."

"Well?"

"Well, what?"

"You have an obligation to preserve this building's history.

I'm here to make sure you fully understand that."

While I was fairly sure Dax and I would end up on the same side of the don't-knock-it-down argument, I didn't like the manner in which he made his suggestions. I didn't get a Bleeding Heart Liberal vibe from him, nor did I get Architectural Enthusiast. What I got was Politician with a side of Short Man Syndrome. "What exactly would you advise me to do?"

He looked shocked at my question. "Apply for historic building status, of course. You do want it to get recognized, right?"

"Well, of course I'd like Sweet Dreams to get recognized for its contribution to Dallas history, but I'd like to get inside first. See the condition of the interior and decide what I'd like to do with it from there."

"What do you mean, what you'd like to do with it? Once the building is granted historical status, you can't make any changes to it. You'll be in violation of the terms."

"To be honest, I don't think there's much of a market for seventy-year-old sewing rooms."

I said it as a joke. Tex could tell it was a joke; I saw him laugh. But Dax did not appear to find humor in anything I said.

"It would be irresponsible for you to consider making changes to the building. If you do, you're throwing away history. Just like everybody else. If you don't apply for historic status, I just—I can't—there are no words." He thrust a stack of paperwork at me. "We're counting on you to do the right thing, Madison." He stormed away.

Rocky looked up at me with his big brown eyes and whimpered. I scooped him up and stroked his fur. "Can you believe the nerve of that guy?" I asked Tex.

"I would have assumed that kind of thing was right up your alley."

"Come on, Captain, you know what they say about assuming things."

The sun was already painting the neighborhood in bright rays that reflected off the non-broken windows of Sweet Dreams, making it hard to look at directly. Standing by a white news van that was parked along the property line was Sid, the friendly neighborhood protestor. Unlike Dax, Sid had the decency to look embarrassed. He said something to the motley crew with him, and they stood up in turn and righted their picket signs.

"I don't understand how all these people knew we would be here," I said.

Tex didn't answer. I looked from the small group of protestors to Dax Fosse to the news van parked by the sidewalk to Tex, and then it hit me. There was only person who could have told them about our arrangement.

"Captain Allen, can I talk to you for a moment? Privately?" I turned around and walked several yards away from the building. I didn't check to see if Tex was following until I felt I was far enough out of earshot of Dax. When I turned around, Tex was a few feet behind me.

"Slow down, Night. I thought you had a bum knee. When did you start walking so fast?"

"Take it up with the grievance committee. You and I made plans to walk through this factory. Twelve hours ago. I thought that was a confidential conversion and that you had the same interest in doing this as swiftly and silently as I did. What changed?"

He crossed his arms. His suit jacket sleeves rode up, exposing the white cuffs of his shirt. His Swiss Army watch peeked out from below the cuff on his left wrist. "No matter how quiet you wanted this thing to be, there's no way this wasn't going to become a news story."

"*You* called them. You're the reason the reporters and the protesters are here. You could have warned me."

"I thought it would be a lot more fun to see the look on your face when the news van showed up." He glanced at my outfit. "I did tell you to wear something special."

"You knew? Last night when you were at my house, you knew you were going to pull this stunt?"

"Night, give me a little credit. This is good for both of us. You said you wanted to do something with the building, right? Don't act so surprised. Technically, it was your idea. People love this kind of thing. It builds up a little drama. They'll follow the updates and talk about it at work instead of politics. They'll feel invested in the progress. It's good press." He reached over and ruffled the fur on Rocky's head. "Bringing Rock was a stroke of genius."

"You did all of this for me," I said suspiciously.

"Not entirely."

"What's in it for you?"

Tex pulled off his sunglasses and looked down at the grass for a moment. When he looked up at me, all traces of humor were gone. "It's not a good time to be a cop. The public distrusts us, and the city wants to cut our budgets. Morale is down, has been down, for a while now."

"How long is 'a while'?"

He didn't answer my question, and I suspected I knew the answer. It seemed the whole world had changed in the past year. Tex had traded the day-to-day autonomy of being a lieutenant in the homicide division for the politics of being the captain, and with that came a whole different set of challenges.

I'd first learned of his promotion while I was in Palm Springs, and the idea of Tex being stuck in an office hadn't been easy to imagine. Now that I was back in Dallas, I saw how often he took the opportunity to get out in the field. Captain

Washington had been happy to sit behind a desk, funneling calls from the mayor, deputy inspector, and special-interest groups, and speaking at the occasional press conference. His staff handled the face-to-face interaction with the public, at least until a situation had forced him to get his own hands dirty to protect his department's reputation. He'd retired shortly after that. I wondered if he'd seen the writing on the wall.

"What's the deal here? Do I have to let those guys in? And the news crew? Is this like an episode of *Ghost Hunters*?"

"It would be easier to let them in, sure, but you don't have to. If you tell them to wait out here, you're probably going to read an op-ed piece about your refusal to cooperate in the news later today. That Fosse guy will make a statement about your intent to destroy the history of Dallas and the Krumholtz guy with the picket signs will come back with signs that say 'Down with Night.' Uh-oh."

"Uh-oh, what?" I turned around and looked the direction Tex was staring. Sid was talking to the news crew. He held a picket sign with the slogan "Pull back the covers on the truth!"

"Wait here," Tex said. He left me standing by the front doors and approached the cluster.

No good could come from this.

I waited by the front door of the factory with Rocky and watched Tex talk to the group that had collected. Sid looked angry; the newsman looked bored. A few more words were exchanged, and then they all turned and looked my way.

I shifted my attention to Rocky, who was digging in the flower beds. I didn't want to be the center of attention, not over this. But between the preservationists, the picketers, the PR needs of the Lakewood Police Department, and the local news crew, I was in the middle of something I couldn't ignore.

A few minutes later, Tex returned to where I was standing. "Okay, Night, I bought you a couple of hours. A day, tops. The news is going to run some background info on the building and a couple of interviews with those guys." He pointed at Sid. "For now, your name stays out of it. Sid will be back tomorrow with more picketers. News at six. Chances are Alice Sweet's family won't be all that happy about your role in dredging up the family history either."

"I'll explain it to them. John asked me to help plan the memorial service. I'll reach back out and tell them face to face."

"It's your call, Night. You can go the easy way or the hard way. What would Mrs. Sweet tell you to do?" Tex asked.

I looked at Sweet Dreams pajama factory, backlit by the rising sun. For one tiny moment, the deterioration of the exterior was hidden behind the kind of glow that inspires thoughts of a higher power. I was moved by the enormity of the past and the confidence Alice had invested in me by leaving me the keys to her family's secret.

"She'd tell me to take the hard way," I said.

Tex grinned. "I was hoping you'd say that."

TEN

Tex, Rocky, and I slowly approached the front doors of the factory. "You do know there's a very good chance the only thing left in there is a room full of rat droppings, right?" he asked.

"I can't think of anybody I'd rather discover rat droppings with than you." I smiled sweetly.

He handed me the key, and I unlocked the padlock. He rearranged the chains until they dropped from the doors, and we went inside. If I'd had any doubts that this had at one time been a working pajama factory, those doubts vanished the second my red canvas sneakers stepped onto the worn wood floors. I bent down and unclipped Rocky's leash, and he trotted in front of me to sniff the unfamiliar setting.

In front of me sat row upon row of workstations with dusty sewing machines. A few had been covered by fabric remnants. I walked up to the closest one and walked a full circle around it. An industrial-sized spool of thread, probably white at one time, was still sitting in place, though the strand of thread from the spool had long since disintegrated.

Large canvas bins on wheels sat between workstations, and mismatched yardage of fabric rested inside. Prints that were at one time bright and colorful were now coated in dust with a gray tinge. I looked at the lower-level windows that were boarded shut. While Tex had been right about the evidence of critters, there was nothing to suggest sunlight had penetrated the workspace for over sixty years.

I walked up and down the aisles between machines with Rocky staying close to my ankles. The interior of the factory was grand, and I could almost hear the camaraderie amongst the seamstresses while they were completing their daily workload. An old vending machine sat, abandoned, along one wall outside of an office labeled Management. That would have been George's office. Close enough that he could keep an eye on the workers but still removed enough that he could close his door to maintain a safe distance.

"What do you want to do with this place?" Tex asked.

"I don't know. I wanted to see what it was like inside before I decided anything."

"Go. Look around. I'll watch Rock."

I walked across the room to a set of large sliding doors. It took a little effort, but I was able to slide one to the side. Beyond the doors was a separate room filled with floor to ceiling cubes. Each cube was filled with colorful items individually bagged in plastic. They were colors normally reserved for candy stores: bubblegum pink, mint green, peppermint blue, and butterscotch yellow. Bags of lavender polka dots, red and white stripes, and orange flowers all begged to be discovered. I pulled one of the bundles out of a cube marked "M" and tore the plastic open.

Inside the package was a flannel nightshirt: white with small colorful conversation hearts printed on the fabric. A shiny white hangtag dangled from the cuff of the garment: Sweet Dreams $4.90. I held it in front of me when it hit me where I was. The inventory closet of the factory. This was where the product went when it had finished being sewn, bagged, and sorted by size, waiting to be sold and shipped to a department store. I slowly rotated in a circle and took in the enormity of the collection. Not only had George closed the business, but he'd left the inventory where it was. The plastic had preserved the garments from whatever elements and critters could have ruined them after all this time.

I wasn't just the owner of a building. I was the owner of possibly the largest collection of New Old Stock pajamas in the country!

I turned around and saw Tex watching me from the back of the room. He leaned against the wall, arms crossed, feet shoulder-width apart. Rocky lay on the floor next to Tex's feet, paws out front, furry little chin propped on top of them. Tex's silence was more unsettling than if he'd belittled my fascination with post-war PJs.

"It's amazing, don't you think?" I said. "It's a time capsule. It's like everybody left at the end of their workday and expected to come back the next day. Only they didn't."

I returned the nightshirt to the inventory bag and placed the bag back in the cubby. I left the inventory room. The first floor was grand, housing four rows of sewing stations with eight machines in each row. I wove between the stations toward the back of the room, where a large black piece of iron equipment was positioned. It was the size of a car, equipped with flutes and pipes and chains to operate it. On the floor under the bottom was a series of pedals. It only took a second before I recognized it as the steamer that had malfunctioned and caused the burns that ultimately led to Suzy Bixby's death.

I stared at it for a few seconds. This machine was at the heart of the drama that had destroyed what Sweet Dreams once stood for by taking the life of a promising young model. It had cost George Sweet his company and had left hundreds of young professional women out of work at a time when they'd relied on their incomes. In the past several years, I'd seen destruction caused by greed, desperation, and mental instability. But knowing how much damage had come from a simple equipment failure was different. There would be no justice. A machine could be dismantled but not punished. George had done the only thing he could: he'd shut down production so the machine would never be in operation again.

I was on the verge of bestowing mythical powers onto an inanimate object, and I didn't like that. I reached out and dragged my fingertips over the surface. Small trails cut through the buildup of dust. I picked up a wad of fabric that rested on the side of the monstrosity and wiped off more dust, exposing dull black iron. I shook the fabric out, and several small silver items fell to the ground like a handful of loose change.

I jumped. And then, as my brain processed what I was looking at, I froze. I could explain the buildup of dust, the abandoned bins of fabric, and the disintegrated thread in the factory. But I couldn't explain the small metal shell casings that had been bundled up inside a scrap of fabric on top of the steamer.

"Captain? I think you should see this."

He crossed the room at a normal pace but slowed considerably when he saw the silver shells. He put one arm out and held me back.

"It's a little late to worry about corrupting a crime scene," I said. "Those bullets have probably been here since before we were both born."

He bent down and peered at one of the shell casings.

"Sorry, Night, you're wrong. These bullets match the caliber of the gun you found in your friend's storage unit. And as weird as it seems, that's not the part that worries me."

"There's something else?"

Tex nodded. He pulled a clear plastic bag out of his pocket and shook it a few times so it opened. He then put his hand inside, picked up the shells, and turned the bag inside out around them. He used the bag to scoop up two more that had been resting behind the leg of the steamer. "At least three of them were ejected from their casing."

"I think you're telling me a gun was fired in this factory within the past week, but I'm having a hard time processing what that means." Tex stared at me intently. His brows were low over his narrowed eyes. I hadn't done anything wrong and didn't like the feeling that I was being scrutinized. "What?" I asked.

"Somebody's setting you up." He pulled out his cell phone, switched the camera to video, and scanned the steamer and the floor around us.

"Don't play with me, Captain. What am I being set up for? Violating a spool of thread?"

Tex looked over my shoulder toward the stairs in the corner. Slowly I turned and faced the same direction. So far we'd only seen a portion of the factory, and I had a feeling it didn't begin to touch the scope of my inheritance. I took Rocky's leash from Tex and looped it over the ballast of the banister. Silently, Tex and I ascended the staircase.

We found the body of John Sweet on the second-floor landing.

ELEVEN

John Sweet was propped up in the corner of the stairs. A small black pistol like the one I'd found in Alice's storage locker rested in his hand. I doubted he'd fallen in that spot. If suicide was initially a possibility, the careful arrangement of his body immediately discounted it. I stared at the floor. Unlike the first level, it was free of dust and debris. Whoever was responsible for John's death hadn't simply shot him and walked away. They'd cleaned up any evidence of what had happened.

The idea turned my stomach. I raced past Tex, down the stairs, past Rocky. I bent over the first receptacle I found, which was the large bin of fabric in the aisle. I threw up the banana I'd eaten that morning, thankful I hadn't eaten more. I felt a hand on my shoulder and jumped. Tex held out a bottle of water.

"I called it in. You're going to have to wait out front."

I took a swig of water from the bottle and swished it around my mouth, and then looked for a place to spit. Tex tipped his head to the same bin of fabric that held my former stomach contents. Might as well.

"That's John Sweet," I said after I'd wiped my mouth. "He's Alice's grandson. He's the one who met me here to tell me about the inheritance and who gave me the letter with the key to the storage unit."

"When's the last time you talked to him?"

"Yesterday. He called to talk to me about the memorial."

"What time?"

"Morning." I kept one hand on the bin of fabric to steady myself. "Give me a second. I'll come back up there with you."

"Sorry, Night. This is no longer a walk through a time capsule. It's a crime scene. That means you and Rock have to get out."

"Are you going to call me later and tell me what you found out?"

"Not my job."

I pointed toward the door through which we'd come. "There's a news crew out there. As soon as I exit this building, they're going to start asking questions. What do you want me to say?"

"Use your judgment." He crossed his arms.

I picked up Rocky, who had been bounding around my feet, and carried him outside.

I knew Tex was right. I knew it. But that didn't make me like the situation any more. I had respect for Tex and the task ahead of his department, but I still hated the feeling that I had nothing to contribute to his investigation.

Sid was in front of the building with the newsman. "What happened?" he asked when I walked past him. "Did you find something? Evidence? I knew it! I'm calling the rest of the Truthers. No, I'll tell them later. I'm going inside."

"No, you're not," Tex said from the front doors. In the background, sirens grew closer. I didn't stick around to see how it all played out.

I drove away from the factory. I was on fire, but not because of the bright sunlight. Anger, helplessness, fear, and a mounting sense of despair blended into a level of anxiety that left my hands shaking on the steering wheel. I drove without knowing where I was going. Before I knew it, I was parked outside of the law offices of Stanley & Abbott.

John Sweet had been alive as recently as yesterday when he

called about Alice's memorial service. He'd had her house keys on his desk the day he'd handed over the letter she left me and said he was making up a second set that I could pick up today. I didn't know how long his body had been at the factory, or why someone had killed him. He shouldn't have even been at the factory. There were so many things I didn't know about what I'd just seen. My brain sent up a warning flare. Alice's death, though unwelcome, wasn't entirely unexpected due to her age and declining health. And Suzy's death, while unfortunate, had taken place before I was born and had been ruled accidental.

But John was a healthy professional on his way to becoming a lawyer who'd been interested in executing his grandmother's estate and collecting his inheritance. True, he'd seemed a little annoyed that a stranger had been given what he'd expected would become his, and his specialty hadn't been estate planning, but he'd let his boss oversee the various job machinations to eliminate the appearance of impropriety. And now he was dead inside the factory he'd told me was mine.

I got out of my car. Rocky followed me across the driver's side and stood on his hind legs with his paws on the door. I didn't plan to be more than a minute or two, but I wasn't willing to leave him alone. I opened the door, and he stepped down. Together we approached the front doors of Stanley & Abbott. They were locked. Inside, Frannie, the same woman who had been vacuuming the day I'd assisted with the broken printer, was running her vacuum over the lobby carpet. I pointed to the doors and then clasped my hands together in a *please* gesture. Frannie switched off the vacuum and pushed the doors open.

"Hi," I said. "I'm a client of the firm. I left a set of house keys here yesterday. John told me I could pick them up today. Is he here?"

"Nobody's here," she said.

"If nobody is here, how'd you get in?"

"The doors were unlocked, and there was a note on them. I figured John had to run out for something, but he knew I was scheduled to come here."

"Has that ever happened before?"

"No. Seemed a little strange, if you ask me."

"Do you have the note?"

"I crumbled it up and took it out with the trash. That's my job."

She looked at me like she wasn't sure if she should trust me. I stood up a little straighter, forced a smile, and willed Rocky to be at his cutest. All I could think about was that someone had wanted John dead. Someone who connected him to the pajama factory. And that my name was on John's calendar and in a file as the inheritor of the factory. John had died because of my inheritance and I had to know why.

Frannie's eyes took in my red and white windowpane dress with the patch pockets and then returned to my face. "Come on in," she said. "It's creepy being here all by myself. I keep feeling like somebody is watching me."

The hair on the back of my neck stood up. Somebody very well might have been watching Frannie—watching both of us— at that very moment. I couldn't just collect the keys and leave her alone. There was no way I would walk away and leave this woman in a potentially dangerous situation, even if it meant Rocky and I were walking into a trap.

I entered. "To tell you the truth, I talked to Mr. Stanley about a job here," I said. What? It wasn't completely a lie. "Can you tell me anything about the men who work here? Anything that might help my chances of being hired?"

She shook her head. "They don't talk very much, not to me, or to each other. Things were different before Mr. Abbott died last year—he was the other partner. Used to have pretty girls working for him, but they'd always quit."

"Why? What did he do?" I asked, making small talk.

"He was a pervy old man. He used to stand behind his secretaries and put his hands on their shoulders, give them massages when they were typing up memos. I could tell they hated it. Anybody who was paying attention could tell. I caught one crying in the bathroom. The next week, she was gone, and the new guy was here."

"John," I said. "Tall, thin, light orangey-brown hair, right?"

"Yeah, that's the one." She laughed. She unplugged the vacuum cleaner and wound the cord around the side. "The universe has a funny sense of humor."

Something about how she said that made me take notice. "What do you mean?"

"John is, you know." She dropped her voice. "Two weeks after he got the job, he threatened the partners with a lawsuit over sexual harassment. He claimed the other partner made inappropriate suggestions when he learned John was"—she dropped her voice—"gay."

"You say the other partner died last year?"

She nodded. She looked over her shoulders as if in fear of being caught spreading gossip. "I don't know what happened with the lawsuit, but John's sexual harassment claims could have burst the dam of what the former secretaries kept secret. He started here as the secretary, but if Mr. Stanley or Mr. Abbott did one thing wrong, John probably could have owned the firm."

While Frannie talked, I walked around to the back of the desk and tried to open the top drawer. It was locked shut. I tried another drawer. Same thing. I looked up and found her watching me.

I dropped into the chair and thought about what she'd said. It sounded like Stanley & Abbott were boys-club lawyers who hadn't adapted to the changing times. They'd had a long run of sexual harassment, at least until John arrived. Even I'd experienced the stereotypical assumptions of Mr. Stanley the day I first came to the firm.

Having John around must have left the partners uncomfortable, especially after John took legal action against them. And after establishing the firm and then maintaining it for decades, the idea of a fresh young face coming in and threatening to take it all away would have left a bad taste in anyone's mouth.

I wanted to get out of the law offices. "Frannie, how long until you're done for the day?"

"I just finished the common areas," she said, and then added, "John asked me not to clean their offices unless they're here. Something about compromising client privilege."

I already knew John wasn't coming back. "Where is Mr. Stanley?"

"I don't know. I thought one of those men would be back by now. I don't feel right leaving the place before they return. You didn't find your keys, did you?"

I tapped the desk drawer. "John put them in here," I said, "but the drawer is locked. I could wait until Mr. Stanley comes back and ask him, but I don't think that's going to look very good for my potential job here."

She narrowed her eyes at me. "I know where Mr. Stanley keeps the master keys. I'll unlock the drawer so you can get your keys, but you have to leave when I do."

"Of course," I said. "Thank you." I stood up to follow her.

"You better wait out here. It'll only take me a second."

I felt like I was in a horror movie. Maybe Frannie had just been imagining the sense that she was being watched, but I couldn't shake the idea that there was something very wrong about the law firm having been unlocked when she arrived.

I picked up Rocky and crept into the hallway behind Frannie. She opened the second door on the left. "Why is it so cold in here?" she said. "Mr. Stanley! I didn't know you were in the office. Why are you working in the dark?"

He wouldn't be. Which meant one thing.

I ran after her and barged into the air-conditioned office just in time to see the body of Mr. Stanley tip forward from his chair and face-plant onto his desk.

TWELVE

Frannie screamed. I set Rocky on the chair opposite the desk and put my hands on the senior law partner's shoulders. It took both Frannie and me, but we pulled Mr. Stanley back into an upright, sitting position. His skin was cold to the touch. His eyes stared forward. A round hole was in the middle of his forehead. I didn't need to check his pulse to know he was dead.

I did anyway.

It's not a good feeling to recognize that in a situation like this, you're the more experienced one. I turned to Frannie, who had lost all color from her face. "Go out to the front desk and call 911," I instructed. "Tell them your name and where we are. Tell them what we found."

"I can't," she said. "I need this job. I support three kids, and I can't afford to be fired. I have to get out of here."

"You can't leave. Neither of us can. Nobody is going to fire you because of this."

She pressed the master keys into my hand. "I can't take that chance." She turned around and ran out of the building.

Where I'd been too worried about Frannie to leave her alone, she apparently had none of the same compunctions about me. I didn't like it here in the offices of Stanley & Abbott. I didn't want to stay here. I wanted to leave as badly as she did, but I had a responsibility now.

I picked up the receiver to the phone on Mr. Stanley's desk. There was no dial tone. I followed the cord to the jack. It had been ripped out of the wall.

Mr. Stanley was beyond the need for protection. I wasn't. I scooped up Rocky and went down the hall to the front desk. This phone worked. I called emergency and reported the body. They instructed me to wait where I was. I looked out the front doors and saw Frannie huddled in the front seat of her car. I admired her for staying despite what she feared about her job security.

While I waited for the arrival of the first officer on the scene, I stayed in the front lobby of the law firm. The offices were silent, but that did little to remove my fears. I didn't know enough about rigor mortis to guestimate how long Mr. Stanley had been dead. His office had been cold, colder than the rest of the building. Residual chills from the experience ran down my spine. I wrapped my arms around my body and rubbed my arms to make the gooseflesh go away. More than anything else I wanted to go outside and stand in a patch of sunlight to warm myself up.

The master keys that Frannie had gotten from Mr. Stanley's office sat on the desk in front of me. They were already covered in my fingerprints from having carried them this far. If the keys with my name on them were inside the desk drawer, I wanted them out. I'd tell Tex and take whatever lecture or punishment came my way, but I wasn't going to become collateral damage in whatever was happening around me. I unlocked the drawer. There were two smaller sets of keys inside the drawer. *Madison Night* was written on a small disc that hung from the silver keyring on one set. I picked both sets up and dropped them into my handbag. I locked the drawer with the master keys and waited with Rocky on my lap.

The first officers and paramedics arrived a few minutes apart from each other. I pointed down the hall and told the paramedics where they'd find Mr. Stanley. Officer Sirokin waited with me in the lobby. He didn't ask me any questions, and I didn't volunteer any information. Aside from the grunting and small talk of the paramedics down the hall, the building was silent.

Tex was the last person to arrive. He walked in and scanned the interior. I waited for him to look at me, but he didn't. I knew he'd get to me in time, and I was on edge until that happened. He consulted with Sirokin and then with the paramedics. When he finally got to me, I wasn't sure what to expect.

"Alice Sweet's memorial service was never planned. The cemetery is burying her today."

"Right now?" I asked.

He nodded. He put his hand on my arm in a comforting gesture and spoke in a soft, soothing tone. "You can leave here as soon as I take your statement. What do I need to know?" he asked.

We stared at each other for a few moments. I considered the many ways I could answer the question. There were facts, and there were rumors. And if I was going to get to the cemetery before Alice's casket was put into the ground and covered with dirt, I was going to have to stick to the facts. I didn't know why being at the cemetery so Alice wasn't buried alone was so important to me, but it was. It was the only thing I could focus on.

"When I arrived, the offices were empty except for the cleaning lady. Her name is Frannie. She's in her car in the parking lot, and she's scared she's going to lose her job over this, though she did nothing wrong. You can get a statement from her and I'm sure it will match mine. She's the one who found Mr. Stanley's body. She went into his office for the master keys and screamed. That's when I went in. The office is cold, like the A/C was left on high. Your team will be able to confirm all of this."

"Why are you here?"

"John was having a set of keys made for me, and after what

you and I found this morning, I wanted to make sure they weren't left lying around."

"Did you find them?"

I reached into my handbag and pulled out the set with my name on them. Tex held out his open palm, and I dropped them in.

"That it?"

"Frannie told me some rumors about the office."

"We'll talk about the rumors later." He pointed toward the door. "Go to the cemetery. I'll be in touch."

I left the law offices and got into my car with Rocky. I drove a mile away from the site and then pulled over to the side of the road to calm down. It was two hours earlier in California. Hudson would be at his job site, but I needed to hear his comforting voice.

"Hey, Lady," he said. The sheer fact that he answered my calls the same way every single time was like a dose of calm. I closed my eyes and pretended I was right there with him.

"Hi," I said.

"You don't usually call during work hours. Everything okay?"

"Not really." I pictured John Sweet's body on the landing of the pajama factory and Mr. Stanley's body inside his office. I told myself there was nothing Hudson could do from California that would change what had happened or what I'd seen. "That's kind of why I called. Can you—can you distract me for a few minutes? Tell me about your life out in California. How's the job going?"

"Jimmy's got the job under control. I drove up to Hollywood yesterday morning and had a couple of meetings. Weird town. You should hear these people pitch ideas."

I leaned back against the interior of my car and cuddled Rocky against my chest. He responded to the sound of Hudson's voice coming through the phone and nosed the screen. I put the call on speaker, but the passing traffic quickly drowned out Hudson's voice. I took the phone off speaker and caught the tail end of his sentence. "...are our names."

"I didn't catch that," I said. "What about our names?"

"I was saying the producers want to change everything that happened in Dallas and just about the only thing left in the script are our names."

"I guess that's something."

"Yeah. That woman who came by your studio might know more than I thought. The latest pitch had a romance between me and Officer Nasty." He laughed, as though that were funny.

"Why you?"

"They have her as the officer investigating the case. Thought that would give it a different slant. Female lieutenant. Apparently strong female leads are hot right now. In their version, she's the sister of the victim."

"What about Tex?"

"There is no Tex."

"How can there be no Tex? He was just as involved as everybody else."

"They think it'll play better with one clear leading man, and that's me."

"Am I in there anywhere?"

"Sure. You're one of the blondes." He laughed again. "Listen, this isn't a great connection. How about I call you later? By then Rocky might be a cat."

I ran my hand over Rocky's fur and felt unwelcome emotions well up within me. "Sure," I said. "I'm not sure what my afternoon is going to be like, but I'll be here."

We hung up. The anxiety I'd felt that morning returned. I'd wanted my conversation with Hudson to act as a distraction from the crime scenes I'd seen, but it had the opposite effect. I felt unsettled and alone.

And angry. And I knew why.

For the past year, I'd been giving away pieces of myself. First when I sold the apartment building that had been my sole source of income when I moved to Dallas. It hadn't felt like a loss because Hudson had been the buyer and giving up the building felt like a small price to pay for what I gained in terms of a relationship. But with Hudson in California and me in Texas, the relationship felt intangible.

My usual MO when life got difficult was to throw myself into work. Mad for Mod had been born out of a love of midcentury design and a desire to lose myself in a different era, but there was no escaping reality. And with business demands growing more difficult every day, I'd hired Connie to help. Mad for Mod was no longer my refuge. Alice's death had come at a time when I least expected it, and while on some level I knew an eighty-six-year-old woman only had so much life left in her, I'd wanted to believe she'd be around forever. I hadn't even had a chance to say a proper goodbye, not to her, and not at the memorial service that had been promised but had never taken place.

I felt like pieces of myself were blowing away, like fuzz from a dandelion that gets caught in a gust of wind. My apartment building belonging to Hudson. Mad for Mod being managed by Connie. Alice's death left my morning swims lonelier than before, and now Tex was keeping me away from the one thing she'd given me to remember her by. If I couldn't grab hold of something, I feared those pieces of me would be lost forever.

I drove to Greenwood Cemetery. The sun was strong, but I couldn't get warm. Rocky sat on the passenger-side floor, curled in a ball. Every time I looked down at him, I found his large round eyes staring right back up at me. He'd seen every horrible thing I'd seen that morning. He couldn't know what it all meant, but he seemed to sense how I felt.

Greenwood Cemetery was a picturesque graveyard that had been funded with money from a Republic of Texas Grant. Started in the late 1800s, it sat in a part of Dallas called Uptown. Though it remained one of the most eerily peaceful landmarks in the city, it went largely underappreciated by the urbanites who preferred wine bars, gourmet taco stands, and cupcake shops that moved into and out of the neighborhood with alarming frequency.

I parked my car in a space outside of the black wrought-iron fence and led Rocky to the gates. Confederate flags marked graves of soldiers who had fought for the South, but beyond them, in a quiet corner, was a newly turned plot. A small headstone read, "Alice Sweet 1932-2018." For everything Alice had been in her life, her tombstone lacked the words to describe her accomplishments or what she'd meant to others. I looked at the plot next to hers, expecting to see George's name. But instead, there was a vacant space. Alice, step-grandmother, stepmother, friend, and wife, had been buried alone. Something about that hit me harder than the two dead bodies I'd seen that same day.

The same shaking I'd felt at the pajama factory came back, this time in my upper arms first, traveling down to my hands. My legs shook too, barely able to keep me standing. I dropped down to the grass alongside the freshly turned dirt and felt tears run down my cheeks and drip onto my polyester dress. Despite our age difference, Alice and I had been friends because we understood each other's choices. I never once questioned why she hadn't remarried. She never once questioned why I was more interested in protecting my own life than in sharing it with someone else. Both of us, through circumstance, had become self-centered in a way strangers didn't understand. I wasn't focused on me because I thought I was more important than the rest of the world. I was focused on me because I felt invisible. I had no legacy for when I died. My company would dissolve. My inventory would become garbage. Nobody would remember the woman in the out-of-fashion clothes from the sixties who picked up discarded furniture from street corners before the trash pickup came.

For the first time in years, I felt my loneliness to my core. Kneeling on a fresh grave only hours after someone I'd known had been buried acted like a portal to all the suppressed emotions over death and destruction I'd never properly released. My parents. Past loves. Victims around Dallas who were little more than names in a newspaper. The tears flowed freely as I thought of how lonely these last few years had felt.

Deep, deep within me, I knew I wasn't crying over my parents, or Alice, or my first real relationship that had left me too emotionally scarred to open myself up to Hudson, who by all accounts was perfect for me. I was crying for the loss of the person I'd been before all of that had happened. The person who knew how to love and be loved, who knew how to take care of others, who could be a friend and a companion and a soul mate. There was a time when I wanted all those things. The death of those dreams had occurred without me even knowing it. I was less than a year from my fiftieth birthday, and I was more painfully aware of the holes in my life than my life itself.

I cried until there was nothing left: no heartache, no longing, no loneliness. I didn't know how many visitors to the cemetery had seen me on the ground by the corner of Alice's grave. I didn't care. Until today, I hadn't allowed myself to see my future. But today, what I saw came with more clarity than I could have wished for. I wasn't a victim. I was alive, but people in my life hadn't been so lucky. Alice, John, Suzy, Mr. Stanley, and countless others hadn't had a choice about their futures.

When my emotions were spent, I pushed myself up to a

standing position and dusted the dirt from my dress. Blade prints of grass had left my bare flesh with the appearance of fossilized foliage. I ran my hands over my tights back and forth to stimulate circulation and then did the same for my face. I suspected I looked subpar thanks to my meltdown. But what I had lost in terms of tears, I'd gained in terms of perspective. No more feeling sorry for myself. It wasn't too late to change my life. I'd done it once before, and I could do it again. I just needed a direction.

My car keys were caught inside my handbag on the second set I'd taken from Stanley & Abbott. I tugged to free them, and the backup set flew out of my bag and landed next to Alice's headstone.

I had never been the type to believe in signs. I liked to feel I was responsible for whatever I did, that I had control over my decisions. That it had been my choice to leave Pennsylvania after a painful breakup with the man I thought I'd spend the rest of my life with. That I'd been the one to prioritize physical therapy in the ensuing weeks after tearing my ACL while skiing away from him. That moving to Dallas, starting my own business, finding a handyman and ultimately shifting that relationship from professional to personal—all had been at my own behest. But seeing the keys I wasn't supposed to have fly out of my bag and land next to Alice's headstone, right after wondering what I should do next, gave me pause.

I looked up at the sky. "Are you trying to tell me something?"

It was equally possible that the torn ACL led me to morning swims, which led to my friendship with Alice. Which brought me to standing exactly where I was, in the middle of a graveyard, wondering if something I'd done in my past had brought me to where I was today.

To be honest, I could see both sides of the argument.

Rocky retrieved my keys. We left the graveyard and climbed into my car. I backed out of the parking spot and drove toward Alice's house.

It was early afternoon, but cars were starting to back up by the entrance ramps. I headed northwest toward a part of town called Merriman Park and eased my Alfa Romeo off the street and into Alice's long narrow driveway. I'd been here before for social visits, but it had been a while. She lived alone and much preferred to find a local coffee shop where we could spend our time. I quickly learned that "coffee shop" meant "bakery" where Alice could indulge her sweet tooth while pretending she was there for the caffeine.

I pushed aside any lingering sadness over the knowledge that I'd never meet Alice at a coffee shop again and put on my metaphorical Mad for Mod decorator's hat. Entering a newly vacant property was part of my day-to-day routine. Alice had even had me walk most of her house once because she wanted to hear what I saw when I looked at the interior she'd long since tuned out.

I unlocked the front door and stepped onto the terrazzo tile in the foyer. Unlike a property recently staged by a realtor, Alice's house still looked like it had when she was alive. Coats hung from a row of hooks in the hallway, and a tall planter in the shape of a moai sat next to a bamboo table and held umbrellas. I walked through the hallway, past the living room, and into the kitchen.

Alice always said the heart of a house was the kitchen.

I unlocked the door at the back of the house and let Rocky loose in the yard. When I turned back to face the kitchen, it immediately became obvious that she'd been working on her correspondence when she'd died. A wooden box filled with thick ivory stationery sat on the table next to an address book and a sheet of self-adhesive stamps. I walked around to the back of the chair where it appeared Alice had been sitting and looked down at the table.

That's where I saw the letter. It was addressed to me and was eerily familiar. It was a draft of the letter John Sweet had given me at the law office, the one in the sealed envelope with the key to the unit at Hernando's Hide-It-Away that had led me to the gun. I read over the words in the last communication Alice had had for me, and once again I was touched by her honesty and her polite urging of me to live my life without regrets. But something niggled at my brain, something small that I couldn't place. I picked up the page and read it three times before it struck me what was wrong.

The handwriting on the letter on Alice's dining room table wasn't the same as the writing on the letter I'd been given by her now deceased grandson.

THIRTEEN

I reached into my handbag and extracted my folded-up letter. I'd kept it with me since yesterday, since going to the storage unit. I hadn't completely expected to be able to walk right up, fit the key in the lock, and access the contents, and somehow the letter provided enough of an endorsement that I was entitled to be there, simply because it felt like Alice had told me it was so. I unfolded my copy and set it on the table and compared the two letters. The words on the first pages were the same. Which begged the question: why on earth would Alice have asked someone else to rewrite her letter to me instead of using the original?

I folded my letter and put it away, and then fanned out the two pages of the letter on the table. The piece of stationery underneath the top page was different than the one I had. *The accident at Sweet Dreams changed George. He grew distant and emotionally unavailable. His family blamed me, and we grew apart.*

As far as the pajama factory goes, I've had offers over the years, but none was worth me confronting the past. Enclosed is a list of interested parties. I'm quite certain any of them would make a sizeable offer if you decide to go that route. There is nothing in those walls that can hurt me now.

I pulled my copy back out and flipped to page two. That was the page that told me about the storage unit.

That was why Alice's letter had been rewritten. Because

Alice hadn't left me a gun in a storage unit. Alice hadn't left me a storage unit filled with a gun and newspaper clippings at all. She'd left me a personal letter about her life. But someone had felt it was more important for me to know about the building's history than the distance between Alice and her husband's family and I didn't know why.

The envelope from John Sweet had been sealed. My first thought went to John. He was Alice's grandson. He had the keys to Alice's house and knew enough about her will to know she planned to leave me an inheritance. He very easily could have recopied the letter and sealed it to give the illusion of it being a private communication that Alice had intended for me. He could have rented the storage unit, hidden the gun and the newspaper clippings, rewritten the letter, and ensured that it ended up in my hands.

But John was dead. I'd seen the body myself this very morning. If he had done everything I suspected, what had been his end goal? He hadn't gotten away with anything—unless the murder of his boss had been committed with the gun I'd found in the storage unit.

The air conditioner had been on high in the senior lawyer's office. That wasn't because it was hot out. It was because whoever had shot Mr. Stanley had wanted to hide the time of death.

I pulled out my phone and called Tex. "Captain Allen, where are you?"

"Uh-oh, this must be official police business if you're calling me Captain. You didn't find any more bodies, did you? Two in one day already makes you an overachiever."

I ignored his attempt to keep things light. "I'm at Alice Sweet's house in Merriman Park."

"You gave me her keys. You didn't break in, did you? Night, I already have my hands full without you nosing around."

"There was a second set of keys," I said. I waited a moment to see what he'd say about that. When he didn't say anything, I continued. "If you can get away from whatever you're doing right now, I think you should come."

The doorbell rang. Immediately I wished my car wasn't parked so prominently in the driveway. "There's somebody here. I'm going to answer the door."

"I think that's a good idea," he said. "Keep your phone on."

I held my phone by my side and approached the front door. When I opened it, I found Tex standing on the porch. He held his phone to his head. "You can hang up now," he said into the phone.

"Very funny. Are you following me?"

"Don't flatter yourself. I'm investigating a case." He held out his hand. "You have something for me?"

I didn't move. "Why are you investigating this case?" I asked. "You're the captain. You have a whole department of officers whose job it is to go out into the field and investigate cases. You being here suggests you don't have faith in your department, and that's not something you've ever indicated before."

Tex pushed past me, crossed the living room, and went into the kitchen. Rocky came in from the backyard and sniffed Tex's ankles. Tex opened a cabinet and pulled out a bowl, filled the bowl with water, and set it down on the floor. Rocky immediately lapped it up.

"What's going on with you?" I asked a little more gently.

He looked up. "I took this promotion so I could move on with my life. Twenty-five years on the force, working my way up from uniform to detective to lieutenant. When Captain Washington announced his retirement, this was the next logical step."

"Do you like being captain?"

"I don't know how to be captain." He pulled a chair out from the table and dropped into it. "Some guys wait their whole life for this job to open up. Sit in an office behind a desk. Task out the team to handle things from the front line. Fill out reports, form committees, and give press conferences."

I pulled out the chair across from him. Alice's correspondence supplies sat in the middle of the table. "You're not some guys. You're you. Why'd you feel the need to change things if you were happy?"

Tex looked away, staring into the living room. A large turquoise carpet sat on top of recently polished hardwood floors. Along the back wall was a long, low blue floral sofa. The cushions were square and tufted with an oversized round covered button in the center of each. On one side of the sofa was the smoky gray fiberglass bullet planter I'd given Alice last year on her birthday. A wild green spider plant spilled out from inside, cascading tendrils down to the floor. On the other side of the sofa sat a small stack of *Martha Stewart Living*. Alice hadn't lived completely in a time capsule.

I suspected Tex's attention was not on the floral damask of the sofa or the like-new condition of the bullet planter. He was thinking about what I'd asked. When he looked back at me, his clear blue eyes held emotions I rarely saw in them. I felt my heartbeat increase, and my arms felt heavier than they'd been seconds before. Neither one of us said a word, but I knew what he was thinking. Tex had taken his promotion for the same reason I'd changed the nature of my relationship with Hudson. After all we'd both seen, the fear of standing still indefinitely had driven us both to move. To take the next logical step.

It wasn't the time or the place to discuss the merits of logic.

I looked away first. In an effort to shove the elephant in the room to the side and focus on something different, I cleared my throat and tapped my finger on the stationery in front of Tex.

"Remember the letter I showed you? The one I picked up at the law office? John Sweet gave it to me the day he told me about inheriting the pajama factory. It was sealed and the keys to the storage unit were inside."

He nodded. His blue eyes clouded over and his face muscles tightened up. "I remember. What about it?"

"When I came here, I found this table set out exactly as you see it. That looks like the letter I showed you except for two things. One, the handwriting isn't the same as the one I have," I paused and pulled my copy of the letter out of my handbag, "and two, the second page is different."

Tex took my pages in his right hand and picked up the other set with his left. I watched him look back and forth between the two copies, doing exactly what I'd done: checking them against each other word for word. He flipped to the second page of mine and pushed the one on the table aside.

"Which one is her handwriting?"

I shrugged. "I would think the one on the table is hers, but I don't know. I've never seen Alice's handwriting. Is that weird? She loved to get emails, so that's what we did."

He pushed his chair away from the table and stood up. "Here's how I see it. This woman was your friend. She probably gave you a key in case of emergency. That's probably how you let yourself in here, right?"

"Um, right."

"She left you a sizeable inheritance, so it stands to reason you were important to her."

"More to the point, in addition to the pajama factory, she left me the contents of her house. She said her step-family wasn't interested in her style of interior design."

"Shit, Night, why didn't you say so in the first place? Let's go."

"Go where?"

"We're going to search this place until we know which letter is the original."

"And?"

"And more to the point," he said slowly, "we're going to see if we can find a match for the copy."

"We?"

"Why not? You asked me here, right? I'm just helping you out as a friend."

It was surprisingly easy to work alongside Tex. Every once in a while he stopped what he was doing, pointed to a pineapple lamp or a Witco wall hanging, and said, "People are going to pay you for that?"

After the third or fourth time, I said, "One of these days you're going to show me how you decorate, and then we'll talk. Right now, I'm picturing Budweiser murals and a Big Mouth Bass that sings when you hit the On switch."

"Give me a little credit," he said. "It's a Lone Star mural, and the only switches I have are the ones that dim the lights."

"I bet they operate by remote control too."

He grinned.

While Tex nosed around the kitchen, I went down the hall and into Alice's bedroom. A white coverlet was draped over the bed. Small white pompoms edged the cover and hung a couple of inches above the floor. At the head of the bed, blue and white pillows in coordinating shams were stacked against her walnut headboard. I hadn't given much thought to where she'd died, but the pristine condition of the bed told me she'd been up and following her usual routine.

A library book sat on the nightstand. That would have to be returned. I picked up the book and thumbed through the pages. A greeting card fell out. I picked it up from the floor and smiled at the Valentine's Day message and graphics depicted on the front. George didn't die until the eighties, and despite the strain that must have befallen their marriage after the pajama factory closed, I thought it was charming that he'd continued to give her cards for romantic occasions. I opened the card. The message inside was dated February 14, 1972, and below the date was a message written in a neat script that tilted forward. *To Alice, you are my everything. Love, Vernon.*

There was no doubt from its condition that this card had been cherished by Alice over the years. Which left only one question: who the heck was Vernon?

FOURTEEN

I returned to the kitchen. Tex was flipping through an address book. "I found something," I said. I held out the card. "It's addressed to Alice, but her husband's name was George."

He studied the card and then pointed to the table. "Let me see her letter to you."

"Which one?"

"The one you found here."

I picked up the one from the table and handed it to Tex. He read over it and pursed his lips. When he was done, he flicked the paper with his finger. "Do you know who she was talking about?"

I snatched the paper from his hand and read it again, only this time, Alice's words took on a different meaning. *I died a happy woman, having deeply loved two different men before discovering the pleasure of singlehood. I suspect you know how that feels.*

There were two ways to interpret Tex's question, but I was only about to acknowledge one of them. "She was married to George Sweet until he died in the eighties. I just figured the other man was somebody after him."

"That card is dated 1972."

"I'm not an idiot," I said, immediately regretting the snappish tone of my voice.

"Where'd you find this?"

"She was using it as a bookmark in a library book I found in the bedroom."

"Assuming the library book wasn't renewed, that means as recently as three weeks ago, Alice was looking at this card. I'm going to guess it wasn't because it happened to be handy."

"Alice knew she was ill. She'd been to several doctors in the past few months. The stationery on the table tells me she was trying to get her affairs in order. And something she wrote in her letter reads like she wished she'd done things differently. I guess it doesn't matter now if she had an affair. Alice's death has nothing to do with the two victims we found this morning," I said.

"Are you sure of that?"

"Captain, it's hard enough—"

Tex cut me off. "I'm not on duty. Call me Tex."

I continued. "It's hard enough to lose a friend. I'm not going to sit here and let you convince me that someone deliberately hurt her. She was an eighty-six-year-old woman who lived a long happy life. Don't turn her into a murder victim."

"I'm not. In case you forgot, I have enough of those." He held up the old card. "But this woman left you a building that's been sealed for sixty years, and the same day someone gets inside—you—there's a dead body."

"I don't mean to split hairs, but the body was there when we arrived. That means it was the *second* time someone got inside. Have you thought of that? How somebody else got into the pajama factory before us?"

Tex looked angry. "That's exactly my point. Somebody is orchestrating this whole thing. I don't think Alice was a victim of anything other than old age. She was a nice lady, and she had *fantastic* taste in decorating." He raised one eyebrow up and then down. I crossed my arms. "She may have had the best of intentions when she left you that pajama factory, but it seems to me somebody out there saw an opportunity when she died."

"What kind of opportunity? You saw the building. It's been ignored for decades. There's evidence of rats. If Dax Fosse gets his way, the Historic Preservation Society will add it to the registry, and it'll be just like the Pythian Temple. You know, that old building catty-corner to the pajama factory that looks like it's falling apart? That building has an incredible history. It was the first building in Dallas designed by an African-American architect for an African-American organization. The Union Bank took over the building and when the Historic Preservation Society forced them into applying, guess what happened? The bank didn't want to spend the money conforming to the HPS codes of maintenance, so now the building is in horrible shape. But sure, it has a plaque, so everybody should be happy. Is that what you want me to do? Turn Alice's past into a shitty building with a bronze plaque?"

Tex barely even flinched at my language. "Somebody went out of their way to leave you—the inheritor of that building—a gun in a storage unit. That took some doing. That person knew Mrs. Sweet wrote you a letter and he or she rewrote it to send you out to the storage unit to make sure you had a gun and a key. By the time you got to the pajama factory, you had a way to get inside and this time you had access to a weapon. And then, what a coincidence. The first day you went out there, you found the body of Mrs. Sweet's grandson, and he was shot with the same kind of gun you now own."

"But you said yourself the ballistics report shows—"

He held up his hand. "I said the gun couldn't have been used in 1954 when Suzy Bixby died at the factory. Those were old rumors, and probably less than one percent of the population of Dallas believes them even if they remember them. Doesn't matter. She was killed by a machine malfunction, not a gunshot. Accidental death. None of that takes away the fact that the spent shell casings on the floor of the pajama factory this morning match the caliber of your pistol."

"But it doesn't make any sense! I spoke to John after we picked up the gun."

"Exactly. And if I hadn't been with you when you picked up that gun, then whoever planned all this would have made you look like a very strong person of interest in his death."

"You're saying whoever killed John made it look like *I* killed him?" He nodded. "Someone wanted John Sweet dead and found a way to frame me?" I asked. He nodded again. "Which means what?

"Which means you have no idea how lucky you are that I answer your calls."

FIFTEEN

I stopped to think about what Tex suggested. "You're saying if you hadn't seen the gun in the unit the day I called you out to the storage facility, the timeline would have been muddied enough to make it look like I picked up the gun and killed John at the pajama factory afterward. Even our recent phone calls would make it seem like I drew him out there. But why would I do that?"

"He's the grandson of the woman you inherited the property from," Tex said. "He might not have liked that she left it to you."

"That explains why *he* would have shot *me*, not why *I* would have shot *him*."

Tex's expression changed. He'd figured something out that I hadn't. He turned around and left the house, slamming the front door behind him. I watched through the front window, a convex architectural detail that gave the house considerable character from the street but distorted the appearance of Tex and the occasional passing car.

He was on his phone. I watched him speak and then wait. The starburst clock on the wall ticked off seconds, then minutes. Finally, Tex spoke again. Whatever the person on the other end of the phone told him didn't leave him happy.

He shoved his phone in his pocket and came back into the house. "I'm going to need you to come with me to the station," he said.

"Why? We're in the middle of looking for a handwriting match. We can't just leave."

"New priorities. I need to take your fingerprints."

"You have got to be kidding me. I thought you were my Get Out of Jail Free card. You just pointed out how lucky I am that you know the timeline of my gun. You know you had the gun when John Sweet was still alive so there's no way I could have shot him."

"Night, please. There are a whole lot of reasons why I have to do this one by the book. Don't ask questions, just do what I say." He stared at me for another beat. "And you better go back to calling me Captain."

I knew how to handle Tex when he was cocky or flirtatious or sexist or mad. But this Captain Tex Allen in front of me wasn't any of those. This reaction was new. Whatever he'd learned on that phone call, he wasn't going to share. And whatever it was, it was bad news for me.

"I have to get Rocky. He's outside," I said.

"I'll get him."

"No, you won't." I pushed past Tex and went back into the house and directly to the back door. Even before I opened it, the scent of skunk spray turned my stomach. I put my hand over my nose and called out, "Rocky! Come here, boy. Rocky!"

Any other day, I might have laughed at the image of a furry caramel and white Shih Tzu slinking across the backyard with his head low like he'd done something wrong. But the closer he got, the more aware I became that he was the source of the skunk smell. His interest in finding a friend in the backyard had led to an olfactory nightmare.

"What's taking you so long?" Tex yelled behind me.

I turned around. "Rocky got skunked." I scooped up Rocky and the scent transferred onto my dress. "We're taking your car."

Tex eyed Rocky, who I swear looked embarrassed by the smell of his fur. Tex's face softened the tiniest bit, and my anger faltered. "Let's go," he said.

I set Rocky back onto the ground and hooked his leash to his collar. The three of us walked towards Tex's Jeep. The last thing I wanted right now was to sit next to him, but aside from riding in the cargo hold, there wasn't another option. At least the open air would help diffuse the acrid scent.

The Lakewood Police Department was about four miles away. After chewing two anti-nausea tablets, I kept my arms wrapped around Rocky while Tex drove. Neither one of us spoke. He parked in a space marked "Captain" by the front door. On any other day, I would have commented on him having his own parking space. Today, I limited my reaction to an eye roll. Like Rocky, at least Tex had the decency to look embarrassed.

"Am I being booked for something?" I asked.

"You're cooperating with the Lakewood Police Department by voluntarily giving us your prints so you can be ruled out as a suspect in an open investigation. I assumed you'd be okay with that?"

"Are you going to tell me what crime you're ruling me out of having committed?"

"No."

Rocky's scent announced our presence before we were inside the door. The desk officer inside, a Mexican man who looked to be about twelve, cursed. "We don't handle that kind of crime," he said, waving his hand in front of his nose. A second later he saw Tex. "Captain Allen. You brought her in?"

"Garcia, I don't want to hear a word about the dog. I need you to take Ms. Night's fingerprints."

"You want me to run her through Live Scan?" Garcia asked.

Tex shook his head. "Ink and roll is fine."

"Why?" I asked. "What's Live Scan?"

The two men looked at each other. Tex nodded at Officer Garcia, who looked embarrassed at having to explain it to me. "A screen reads your fingerprints and runs them against the known prints in a centralized database. If they match prints from any other crimes, we'll get a hit."

I turned back to Tex. "Captain Allen, may I remind you of a phrase you used in the car earlier? Something about going by the book?"

"Garcia, take Ms. Night's fingerprints and then run her through Live Scan."

"What did she do?" Garcia asked. "Besides cause a public nuisance with her dog."

Rocky whimpered by my leg, like he knew Officer Garcia was talking about him. Tex reached out for Rocky's leash. "I'll take care of Rock."

I knew I could trust Tex, but that didn't make me any less angry with him. I didn't let go of the leash. "If anything happens to my dog, I'll kill you." I held his stare long enough to make my point and then turned to Garcia. "And I say that knowing full well my fingerprints will be on file."

Garcia looked like he wasn't sure what to make of the scene in front of him. Clearly, he was fresh out of the academy.

Tex scooped up Rocky and held him over one shoulder. He kept one hand on Rocky's back and used the other to tug on the leash.

"I mean it," I said.

"I know."

I let go of the leash, and Tex stepped away from us. "Garcia, put her in Interrogation Room Two when you're done. I'll be back in about an hour."

There's only so much small talk you can cover while being fingerprinted by a twelve-year-old officer who seems more afraid of you than you are of him. After Garcia rolled each of my fingerprints onto a ten card and labeled it neatly, he stood me in front of what looked like a small metal box with a green light. The box was connected to an LCD screen mounted on the wall. He put my hand on the flat upper surface of the box, fingertips pointing toward the green light, squishing my fingers together until all the tips from one hand were flat on the exposed surface. As the light beam recorded my prints, they appeared on the LCD screen. Green markers around the border of the screen lit up.

"Is this thing new?" I asked.

"Yeah. Most departments have them. It's changed the way we conduct investigations."

"Because it interfaces with some other agency?"

"Yeah. If your prints were found at a crime scene, we'd get a hit in as soon as ten minutes. It's great when we need a reason to hold somebody." He maneuvered the mouse and clicked a few buttons and then explained that he needed to take finger rolls on the screen surface next.

"Do you need a reason to hold me?"

"Well, Captain Allen said to hold you, but I think that's because he's going to bring your dog back."

"He said to put me in Interrogation Room Two."

"That's what we call the break room. Sounds more official when there are civilians around." Garcia grinned. "Besides, after what you said, he probably knew you wouldn't want to leave without your dog."

That was true. And while Tex knew how to find me, I wasn't about to let on that Garcia's captain and I had anything more than a passing person-of-interest relationship. At least not until I knew what the heck had triggered this sudden shift in Tex's behavior.

"I recognize your name," Garcia said. "It was on the news. You own the building where we found the body this morning, don't you?"

"Afraid so," I said. "I only just inherited it two days ago. At least I think I inherited it. The murder victim was the executor of the estate. I'm not sure what's going to happen now."

Garcia shrugged. "Probably defaults to a different lawyer."

I was trying to figure out the best way to keep Garcia chatting about the events of the morning when he switched off the box that scanned my fingers. "You're all done here," he said. "I don't know what Captain Allen thought he'd find, but I'm going to ask you to wait until he gets back." He looked at his watch. "Shouldn't be too long now."

"Did Captain Allen tell you why I'm being printed? Because as far as I know, I'm here voluntarily to eliminate the possibility that I was involved this morning. I'm sure it's just a technicality since I inherited the building and knew the suspect."

Garcia looked uncomfortable. "Ma'am, I can't talk about that."

"Do I really have to wait in your break room?"

"I have some filing to do, so if you want to wait out here, I think that would probably be okay."

And it would have been okay under normal circumstances. But when the doors to the precinct opened and former detective Donna Nast walked through, followed by her Hollywood replica Erin Haney, I had to admit that Interrogation Room Two sounded an awful lot like Club Med.

SIXTEEN

As soon as I saw the former detective, I stood up from my chair. It wasn't that she instilled fear in me—quite the opposite. That was the thing about Officer Nasty. She was quite the opposite of me, my life, and everything I stood for.

Where I dressed in sweet vintage outfits that coordinated with daisy pins and colorful sneakers, Nasty dressed in tight jeans, revealing tank tops, and stiletto heels. My blonde hair was usually secured away from my face in a neat ponytail or ribbon. My bangs, and a lifelong addiction to SPF 50, made me look younger than the age on my driver's license. But Nasty had golden skin and copper streaks through her long dark tousled hair. Even when she'd been on the force and dressed in uniform, she looked like she'd just rolled out of bed.

Some days she had. And did I mention? Some days, that bed had been Tex's.

These days she ran Big Bro Security, a somewhat opportunistic company which exploited local crimes to generate business. Thankfully, I saw her before she saw me. It was her shadow who blew the whistle on my fade-into-the-background routine.

"Madison?" Erin said. "This is unbelievable! It's a sign. This whole trip has been one sign after another. I'm totally going to get this part."

Nasty whipped around and her hair flew out like the mane of a show horse. "Madison Night? What are you doing here?"

She waved her hand in front of her face. "And what's that smell?"

"I'm waiting for Captain Allen," I said. As soon as the words were out of my mouth, I realized how many different interpretations there could be, especially from her. I smiled inside, knowing I wouldn't mind if she got the wrong idea.

"Um, Ms. Night? I think maybe that's why Captain Allen wanted you to wait in"—he pointed down the hallway—"the other room."

Nasty smiled. "He wanted you in Interrogation Room Two? That's rich."

Erin was delighted by the turn of events. She held her hands out in front of her, making mirror Ls with her index fingers and thumbs like a director framing a movie scene. "I'm just going to stand here and watch you two catch up. Pretend I'm not here. Donna, what were you saying about Madison?"

Nasty turned on Erin. Her fists balled up, and I think Officer Garcia feared for a moment Nasty might have to be restrained. "Need I remind you of our confidentiality agreement?" Nasty said to her. "If you want my help with this, you are to listen and take notes, but anything I tell you is not—I repeat, not—to be shared, or this entire arrangement is null and void."

Erin looked taken aback for a fraction of a second and then snapped out of it and returned to her effervescent self. "Madison, this is great. I've been shadowing Donna for the day, and I asked her if she'd show me the police department."

Nasty looked at Garcia. "Captain Allen knew we were coming. He's not here?"

"He had an unexpected emergency," Garcia said.

"Homicide?"

"Skunk." He jutted his chin out toward me. "Her dog got sprayed."

The Life Scan machine made a beeping noise, and Garcia left the three of us in the lobby and crossed the room to check it out. I watched until his back blocked the machine. While I knew I hadn't done anything wrong, there was the troubling matter of the frame-up that Tex had mentioned earlier, and I found myself wondering how far someone would go to cover their tracks while making me appear guilty.

Nasty turned to me. "I don't want to know what you do for Tex to get him to take care of your skunked dog. I guess this means you're not dating Hudson anymore?"

"Hudson and I are just fine," I said. "He's in California, and I'm here."

"I know. I talked to him this morning. Funny, he didn't mention you."

It felt like someone had used a vacuum to suck the air out of the room. Hudson hadn't mentioned anything about Nasty, either. I put my hand on the chair where I'd been sitting and bent my leg to rest my knee on the worn wood. It felt like a position of weakness, so I pulled my leg back off the chair and stood on both feet, resulting only in making me look fidgety.

The only reason for Nasty to say that was to get a reaction. That was the way she was. And I wasn't going to take the bait. But as soon as I had Rocky, as soon as I was away from the police station, I was calling Hudson to find out what was going on.

"I would ask how you've been, but I heard about the pajama factory on the news earlier today. You sure cause a lot of trouble."

"If you saw the news, you'd know I was the one who found the victim. I was escorted by a police officer on the property that I'd recently inherited, so unless you'd like to contribute something I don't already know, then I think we can agree I'm the more knowledgeable one in this conversation."

At that moment, Garcia turned around and smiled at us. "You're in the clear, Ms. Night," he said.

"You were Live Scanned?" Nasty asked. A slow smile crept across her face. "That changes things, doesn't it?" She flipped her hair over her shoulder and took a deep breath, which succeeded in making her breasts a little more prominent than they'd been seconds before. "Officer Garcia, I'm investigating the death of the attorney who was found today and sure would appreciate some cooperation with the department where I used to work."

The front door opened. Rocky raced in and ran straight to me. Tex came in next. He held a brown paper grocery bag. He caught the tail end of Nasty's request. "Not on my watch," he said.

The funny thing about relationships is that people don't ever really seem to move on completely. Tex and Nasty—that was history. There'd even been a time after they'd broken up when she and I had joined forces to help prove he was innocent of a series of abductions being committed around Dallas. But put the three of us in a room together, and we were right back where we'd started, in that competitive territory when we first established who we were and whether or not we'd trust each other. And Erin Haney stood off to the side taking it all in. I wouldn't have been surprised to find out she'd wired herself with a body cam so she could study us later for her audition.

I didn't have the energy to battle this round, so I sat back down in the worn wooden chair and ruffled Rocky's fur. He smelled faintly of vinegar and tomatoes, an odd combination. The skunk scent was gone, though, a fact I was sure we'd all agree was an improvement.

Nasty dropped her flirtatious act around Tex. I'd never known how serious their relationship had been aside from the fact that, for a short period, they'd shared an address. I didn't know if that had come about because of convenience or romance. For all I knew, one of them could have been having their own place bombed for termites. Yet it troubled me that it had happened at all, and it troubled me that I even cared.

"What's up, Nast?" Tex asked. He set the paper bag on the table and looked past her at Erin and then back to her.

"I'm giving this woman a tour of Dallas," Nasty said.

"I'm an actress," Erin said. "I'm hoping to audition for the part of Donna Nast in the movie they're making about Hudson James. I hired Donna—the real Donna—so I could get into character. You know, see what life was like for her when she was investigating the case."

Tex's face said everything I'd thought when I heard the news. His brows dropped over his eyes, hooding them like an angry emoji. He stared at Erin for a few beats, and then back at Nasty. He shifted his weight slightly, with his feet shoulder-width apart and his thumbs hooked into the front pockets of his jeans. It was the first time I'd noticed that he'd changed his clothes since taking Rocky with him. His suit had probably been ruined.

"This is a police department, not an acting studio," he said.

"Five minutes," Nasty said. "Give me five minutes to show her around the precinct. For old times' sake."

Ugh.

I'd already seen enough unpleasant things today and didn't want to add this one to the mix. It was after dinner, I was starving, and I wanted little more than to hear a comforting voice. "I'm going to make a phone call," I announced to the room. "I trust it's okay with everybody if I step out front for privacy?"

I was met with everything from pity (Erin) to fear (Garcia). Tex nodded once. Rocky and I went out the front doors. The outside air helped diffuse the lingering smell of Pepe Le Pew. I called Hudson.

"Hey Lady," he answered in his soothing drawl. "Your day get any better?"

"I'd have to say the answer to that is no. Did you talk to Officer Nast today?"

"Yes. The screenwriters had a couple of questions about her that I couldn't answer. I called her to see if she was okay with me giving them her contact info. Is that why you're upset?"

"No. I should have known it was something like that. It's this thing with Alice's estate. Remember I told you how she left me a sealed letter?"

"Sure," he said. Unlike our earlier call, tonight the sound quality was clear. I closed my eyes and imagined we were in the same room.

"She left me a letter, but it turns out she didn't write it. I mean, she wrote me the letter, but somebody else rewrote it and added a second page that wasn't from her, but I thought it was, so I followed the instructions and went to a storage unit I thought she opened in my name and found a gun."

"Whoa, calm down." He paused. "Alice left you a gun?"

"Yes. I mean, no. I mean somebody wanted it to look like Alice left me a gun, but she didn't. There was a storage unit opened in my name, and the gun was in it, but Alice didn't do it." I stopped to consider what I knew. "At least I don't think she did."

"You need to call Tex Allen."

"I already did. But now two people are dead, and maybe my gun committed the crimes, and I'm at the police station getting fingerprinted."

"Shhh. It's all going to be okay."

"Is it? Is it all going to be okay? Did you hear me? I was fingerprinted. My fingers are covered with ink, and then they were scanned into a database."

"Tex knows you didn't shoot anybody."

"That's not the point." I looked up at the sky and collected myself. One emotional breakdown per day was already more than my daily quota. "Everything is changing," I said. "It feels like the ground keeps shifting under my feet."

"That's life, honey. If things didn't shift and change, we'd never grow."

"But sometimes I feel like I just want everything to be normal."

"What's normal?"

I opened my eyes. "I don't know. You and me together in the same state?" He was quiet, so I continued. "I don't know how to do this," I said. "You're out there, and I'm here. And I feel like I'm lost. And you're talking to Hollywood about your story, which is fine. It's good. But it's also my story, and you never asked how I felt about that."

"Actually, I did. You told me to get closure."

He was right. It had been a year ago, right about when we'd become romantically involved. At the time, I'd so clearly seen how important it was for Hudson to be able to move on from the circumstances in his past. I felt selfish for even caring, but I also knew if I bottled this up, I'd be resentful.

He spoke again, this time more quietly. "Do you want me to walk away from this?"

"I won't ask you to do that."

"I know you won't. That's one of the things that makes you special. Except I'm starting to wonder what keeps you from asking me."

I stared out at the row of police cars parked in front of the precinct. A metal fence enclosed the lot. The gate pulled aside to let vehicles in and out. A red VW bug drove past, giving me one tiny detail to focus on while I sorted my thoughts. "Doesn't it scare you? That somebody is going to take a piece of your life and make it into something commercial?"

"Madison, just because somebody uses what happened to tell a different story doesn't change anything. They can do what they want. Life goes on."

"But you're so calm about that. How can you be so calm?"

"It doesn't change anything. My life is still my life."

"You don't feel like you're losing something?"

"Can't say I do. It's fiction, Madison. Whatever they do, it's only an illusion. And in a way, watching them spin my life into a movie plot has given me a perspective I never had. I spent twenty years in Dallas, living a life I could respect, trying to avoid the subject. It feels good to have it out in the open."

"I know you're right. I'm sorry to keep calling you and being so emotionally needy."

"Are you going to be okay?"

"I'll survive," I said. "But do me a favor? If they write a romance between you and Officer Nasty, give me fair warning before we go see the movie."

He chuckled. Despite ending the call on an upbeat note, I felt unsettled. Something I'd said felt off, like I knew something I didn't know I knew. I shook my head quickly to ward off the thoughts, the way Rocky shakes his body after a bath, and headed back inside the precinct. My call to Hudson had been intended to make me forget the reason I was at a police station, but it had done the opposite. By repeating the facts to him, I knew Tex was misinterpreting whatever he'd learned during that phone call at Alice's house. And then the piece of information I'd forgotten clicked.

I went back inside the police station. Nasty stood by the Live Scan machine showing Erin how it worked. Tex was ten feet away, by the front desk, with his arms crossed over his chest. Garcia was seated behind the desk typing up a report. The brown bag was gone from the table.

"Captain Allen, can I talk to you?" I asked. I glanced at the two women. They were absorbed in their conversation. "It's about earlier today."

"Not now," he said in an offhand manner.

"But it's important. It's about your investigation."

"Not now," he said again. This time I was the object of his glare.

Fine. I'd already figured out the one fact that had been bothering me, and if Tex weren't willing to listen, then I'd have to get his attention another way.

I approached Officer Garcia. "How long did you tell me it takes for your Live Scan machine to come back with a hit?"

"Fastest we've ever seen is eleven minutes," he said. "Average is about an hour."

I turned to Tex. "Captain Allen, I bet Erin would love to see a demonstration of how the fingerprint machine works. Why don't you show her?" I smiled sweetly. "Consider it a public service demonstration."

Tex stared at me like he knew I was up to something but couldn't figure out what. A few seconds later he looked at Garcia. "Take my prints," he said.

"Yours?" I asked, fighting to keep the surprise from sounding phony.

"I have no reason to scan either of these women," he said.

"Oh, come on, Captain, I'm sure you have a consent form around here somewhere."

"What are you up to, Madison?" Nasty asked.

"Me? I just thought Erin would like a demonstration of the equipment the Lakewood Police Department uses every day."

"Oh, I would!" Erin said.

Garcia switched on the computer and the machine. Tex set his hand below the green light, and the beam slowly scanned in his prints. We all watched them appear on the LCD screen that was mounted on the wall. When both sets of fingertips had been scanned, Garcia proceeded with the finger rolls. Somewhere during the process, Tex shifted from his annoyance over my suggestion to an apparent ease in being able to teach the pretty actress about the equipment.

After the whole process was done, he explained what happened next. "The prints are uploaded into a central database. They're checked against any other prints: unidentified prints that were lifted from crime scenes and those of known criminals."

And then the printer turned on behind Garcia's desk, and a sheet of paper spit out. A red light went on the LCD screen, and a beep sounded.

"What's it doing?" Erin asked.

"Yes, what's happening?" I asked. "It didn't do all that for me."

"That's because your prints didn't get a hit," Garcia said. He picked up the report that had printed and scanned the document. "Captain? You might want to see this."

Tex snatched the piece of paper out of Officer Garcia's hand. He glared at the paper, and then at me.

"I tried to tell you, Captain, but you didn't want to listen," I said. "You asked me to cooperate by voluntarily having my prints scanned in so you could rule out a match on the weapon used to kill John Sweet. Remember?" I gave him my most endearing smile. "But you should also remember I never touched that gun. You did."

SEVENTEEN

"You got a hit on your prints?" Nasty asked. "In an open investigation?" She tried to take the paper from Tex, but he pulled it away from her.

"Everybody out. Nasty, Night, you"—he pointed to Erin—"out. Garcia, get the Deputy Inspector on the phone."

"Right away, Captain." Garcia picked up the receiver to make the call.

"Not here," Tex said.

"Oooh, you should use Interrogation Room Two," I said.

Tex looked at me with fire in his eyes. "Use the phone in my office."

Garcia hung up the phone and went down the hall. I turned toward the door.

Nasty crossed her arms. "Erin, go home. I'll call you tomorrow." She didn't take her eyes off Tex. The fact that he'd called her Nasty in front of the rest of us wasn't lost on me, and I suspected from the look on her face it wasn't lost on her either.

"Both of you go home," Tex said.

"Okay," Erin said.

"I think I'll wait until the inspector arrives. Erin, I'll call you tomorrow," Nasty said.

The actress looked at each of us, her eyes wide. "Okay, I'll wait to hear from you."

She left the police station without a goodbye.

Once the door closed behind her, Nasty spoke again. "I

don't know what's going on around here, but right now there's the appearance of misconduct. As a former member of the police force, I'm the most qualified person here to make sure you act according to proper procedure."

Her words were different, but the sentiment was the same as what Mr. Stanley had said about impropriety at my meeting with John, and what Tex had said about going by the book after his phone call at Alice's house.

I ignored Nasty and took a step toward Tex. "That's it, isn't it? Whoever put the gun in the storage unit figured I'd tell somebody. That's a normal human reaction, isn't it? It's a weird thing to find. Not many people would just pocket the gun and think nothing of it. It just so happened that the person I called was a cop, but I don't think that matters. The only thing that mattered was that somebody's prints got on it. I didn't pick up the gun, but you did. We were the only two people at the storage unit, and we were the only two people in the pajama factory. Somebody was getting set up for murder. It didn't matter who. This isn't personal—it isn't about me inheriting the factory at all. It's about setting up a scapegoat."

Tex and I had seen two bodies today, and that had put them in the order of discovery in my mind. But the air conditioner masked the time of death for Mr. Stanley, and I hadn't talked to John since yesterday morning. Based purely on the facts as I knew them, I couldn't say which death had happened first or what day they'd taken place. Tex already knew my gun hadn't been used to kill John, but what if that's what the killer wanted us to think? No one could have predicted me going from the pajama factory to the law firm for the keys John had made me.

"Somebody wants us to think John shot Mr. Stanley and then shot himself," I said. "Case closed. But you and I both know that's not possible."

Tex raised his eyebrows like he wanted to see where I was

going with my theory. "Walk me through what you're thinking."

"Mr. Stanley's body was at the law firm. John's was at the factory. Nobody knew I would go to the law firm after finding John's body."

"Nobody knew we were going into the factory either."

"What if the gun I found was a plant? Bodies start turning up, I find a gun, it's the same kind that was used in these murders. That wouldn't look good for me, would it?"

Nasty, who had been watching me closely, spoke up. "Ballistics can match a bullet to a gun. It doesn't matter if it's the same make and model. The bullet will have strike marks that match the inside barrel."

I turned to her. My brain was still processing the facts that I knew, and I was more eager to convince Tex of what I suspected than to be bothered by her presence.

"You need to check the scattered shell casings at the factory and see if they match my gun or the gun in John's hand. I know the department resources are overtaxed." I looked back and forth between their faces. "But two identical guns. Two victims, both shot. Somebody used my gun and went to great lengths to hide it. What are the chances they got mixed up? Do bad guys ever pass off guns to innocent people, or does that only happen in the movies?"

Tex and Nasty looked at each other. Neither spoke. I studied Nasty and then switched my attention to Tex. "Your silence is not an overwhelming argument against my theory."

"It could happen," Tex finally said.

"It did happen," Nasty said.

"What happened?" I asked.

"This. Exactly this. A gun given to a supposed innocent person. Lack of evidence. The case was compromised," Nasty said.

"When?"

"A little over a year ago."

Nasty looked at Tex. He watched her, but not in a judgmental way. I could tell there was significance behind the time frame but felt ridiculously out of the loop. I was tired and cranky, and while Rocky smelled faintly like antipasto, my clothes still held traces of skunk. I wanted little more than to go home, take five showers, and climb into bed.

At least until Tex spoke. "It wasn't a homicide investigation. It was a Class A Misdemeanor. The negligence cost us a guilty conviction and a good officer."

"Somebody got fired over it?" I asked.

"It wasn't a fireable offense," Tex said.

"Somebody quit," Nasty interjected. "And that somebody was me."

EIGHTEEN

I knew Donna Nast had left the police force, but I'd come upon the knowledge by accident. What I'd never gotten were details. I doubted she would have given them if I'd asked. Circumstances at the time had given me a sort of tunnel vision. Nasty and I were never going to be friends, but more than once we'd been on the same side of a critical situation. I didn't like her one bit, but I'd never seen her be unethical. If pressed to guess, I would have suspected her break-up with Tex had made employee relations more difficult. The knowledge that she'd quit over an infraction came as a surprise. It also hinted at a more vulnerable side of Nasty, one I hadn't been expecting.

She turned to me. "Don't get any ideas, Madison. I quit for a hundred different reasons and my life has never been better. I own my own company. There are no office politics at Big Bro. My staff knows I'm the boss. We get the job done, and I make twice what I made on the force. I sleep very well at night."

Garcia returned. "The Deputy Inspector wants to talk to you," he said to Tex.

"You wait here and keep them company." Tex looked back and forth between Nasty and me like he wasn't sure what he'd find when he returned. Rocky sat in one of the chairs by the front door. No way was it as comfortable as the ball chair he slept in at Mad for Mod. In his own way, he'd had a pretty stressful day, and I felt sorry for him.

And then I remembered Connie and her girls' night in. I'd

completely forgotten to call her to let her know I wouldn't be there. No wonder I didn't have a lot of girlfriends.

"Excuse me," I said. I walked out of earshot and called. "Connie, it's Madison. I'm at the police station."

"Are you okay? I saw something on the news about the pajama factory and the lawyer's office—"

"I'm fine. Everything is fine. It's just—this day is never going to end, and I forgot about movie night. I'm so sorry."

"Don't worry. I called it off when I saw the news. Joanie's here. She's helping me with my record sleeves. She's a genius. She brought a box of Archie comics from her store, and we're making the sleeves out of them. We're going to make a killing."

I was happy to hear Connie excited about her new project but had serious doubts about the potential profit structure to a business that relied on the gang from Riverdale.

"You're still coming to Mad for Mod tomorrow, right? I'll bring you a sample," she added.

"Right. See you then."

I hung up and turned around. Nasty stood by the door staring at me. "I missed girls' night," I said.

"And I wasn't invited? Darn. I'm due to have my hair braided."

Something about her flip tone, minutes after confessing she'd left her job here at the precinct over an infraction, made me laugh. I didn't want to, but the exhaustion, confusion, and hunger hit me, and it was all I could do. I clamped a hand over my mouth, too late.

Surprisingly, Nasty laughed too. "I don't know what it is about you, Madison, but you tap into my inner mean girl."

"I don't think I have an inner mean girl," I said.

"Really?" She stood right in front of me and turned around, so her perky backside in skin-tight jeans was facing me. She draped her long, streaked hair to one side and looked at me over her shoulder. "What do you think of these jeans?" she asked.

"Those are jeans? I thought they were a tattoo."

She turned back to face me. "There's hope for you yet." She walked behind the front desk and unfolded the top of the bag Tex had brought. Whatever was inside caused her expression to change. She pushed the bag away and opened a small refrigerator. "Are you kidding me?" she said. "There's nothing in here except yogurt, and I'm pretty sure that was mine before I quit." She shut the door.

Garcia opened a drawer to his desk and pulled out a box of protein bars. "Knock yourself out," he said.

Nasty reached in and pulled out two, and then came to the table and offered me one. I took it. She moved to the coffee pot in the corner and filled two cups.

"That's not fresh," Garcia said.

"Do I look like I care?" Nasty answered. She came back and handed me a cup. "You're not a suspect in anything. You know that, right? If Tex thought you did something, you'd be in holding. For him, the job comes first. Period."

"I know," I said. I stared in the direction of the hallway. "There were some questions about a gun used in a homicide today, and I voluntarily had my prints scanned so they could be checked against the evidence."

"There had to be something connecting you to the gun. People don't just walk in and say, 'scan my prints to see if they match evidence in a homicide.' Even people like you."

"I resent the inference."

"I didn't know I made one."

I turned to look at her. Even when she was trying to be nice, she rubbed me the wrong way. "Alice Sweet asked her grandson, John, to draw up her will. She left me the pajama factory and gave John a sealed envelope that we thought might explain her motive. Inside was a letter and a key to a unit at Hernando's

Hide-It-Away."

"Hernando's," she repeated. "That place is shady. I think they rent units by the hour, not the month."

"I found a gun in the storage unit. Until recently, I had every reason to believe the letter, the box, and the gun had been left to me just like the pajama factory. The murder took place at the pajama factory. You said you saw it on the news, remember? It wasn't a stretch for Captain Allen, or anybody, to place me in the middle of this investigation. Scanning my prints was an easy way to take me out."

"Did your prints hit?"

"No."

"Why not? They should have."

"I never touched the gun."

"I don't get it."

"I found the gun. It seemed like an odd thing to find in a storage unit I didn't know I had, so I called Captain Allen. He joined me and took possession of it. When he told Garcia to scan my prints, he probably thought I'd picked it up at some point."

She smiled slowly. "You didn't, but he did. And when he ran his prints to show off for Erin, they came back with a hit. And now he's on the phone with the deputy inspector trying to explain why. I would love to be a fly on that wall." Her smile grew wider, showing off teeth that could only be that white by using Crest Whitestrips more frequently than recommended. My inner mean girl bit back a comment about them glowing under a black light.

I sipped at the stale coffee. There was no way anyone would believe Tex had something to do with the crimes today. His phone call was probably a technicality, and now he was communicating details of the case, maybe even soliciting another professional opinion. But the longer we sat out front, the more curious I became about Nasty's history.

"What happened here?" I asked her. "When you left the force. Captain Allen said it wasn't a fireable offense. Why'd you leave?"

"That's none of your business," she said. "I don't live in the past like you. It happened, I made a choice, and now my life is better. I cut a lot of dead weight when I left. That stupid mistake was probably my subconscious giving me an out."

"You think I live in the past?" I asked.

"Your whole life is the past. The clothes you wear, the houses you decorate, the movies you watch. It's all about what was, not what can be. I'm no shrink, but sure seems to me you're trying to live in a world that doesn't exist anymore."

That was it. I jumped up from the table and Rocky, who'd been curled up at my feet, jumped too. The sudden movement made the table bounce, and my cup of stale coffee splashed onto the splintered surface.

"You know nothing about me," I said. "Decorating and clothes, those are interests. Everybody has interests."

She remained seated and seemed amused at my reaction. "You take 'interests' to a whole other level."

"How many times since you walked in that door have you mentioned that you own your own business? I own my own business too. I moved to Texas with a car filled with my most valued possessions and nothing else. Everything I have is because I cut ties from my past and moved on. If I lived in the past, I'd still be in Pennsylvania."

Just thinking about those days left me shaking. I'd moved from Pennsylvania to Texas to start fresh. I'd bought an apartment building, adopted Rocky, and started Mad for Mod. I'd taken up swimming to stay active and threw myself into volunteer work at the Mummy so I wouldn't have time to think about what I'd left behind. In time, the memories had faded. I thought I'd moved on, but I hadn't. I hated Nasty for bringing it all back to the surface.

She pulled a bunch of napkins out of a wicker basket that sat on the end of the table and sopped up the coffee spill. In my eagerness to deflect what she said, I'd given her plenty of fodder for more verbal jabs. She wadded up the napkins and tossed them across the room into a small metal wastepaper basket. Garcia sat at the desk, staring at his screen and clicking his mouse. He was either more engrossed in Solitaire than anyone I'd ever seen before, or he was doing his best to pretend he, or we, weren't all in the same room.

Nasty sat back and put her hands on the arms of her chair. "Garcia," she said. "Can you give me and Madison some privacy?"

He looked up. "I don't think that's such a good idea."

"Both of our prints are in your database. If one of us kills the other one, it'll be a nice, neat case." She raised her hand from the arm of her chair and made a *shoo* motion. "Go file something. We'll be fine."

It was late at night and, aside from us, the precinct had been quiet. I had my doubts about Officer Garcia's future, but that wasn't my concern. Garcia stood up and said, "I'm going to the evidence closet, but I can still see you from the cameras back there."

"Great. Not sure what you're hoping to see, but let me be clear. Madison isn't my type."

Garcia had the decency to blush. He carried a clipboard and a set of keys to a closet behind the counter, unlocked the door, and then went inside.

"So stupid," Nasty said. "No way he's watching us while we're out here." She stood up and went behind the counter. "I could hack into their system in two minutes. See their open cases and suspect lists." Her eyes danced over the files in the tray next to her desk. "I won't, but I could."

"Why'd you quit?" I asked again, this time more gently.

"I left for a hundred different reasons: rampant sexism. My history with Tex. The polyester uniforms." She flipped her hair over her shoulder and glanced up at me as if checking my reaction. I focused on putting out a non-judgmental vibe. "I saw a chance to start over and be the one in charge and I took it."

"I get all that, but you could have left anytime you wanted. Why did it take an infraction to motivate you?"

"Because the price of my error was too high."

"People make mistakes, Donna. Even Captain Allen said that."

"Yes, but the mistakes people make don't usually drive others to suicide."

NINETEEN

"What happened?" I asked.

Nasty looked up at me and narrowed her eyes. I sensed she was judging my curiosity. I regretted having played into her dueling mean girls trap earlier. That wasn't who I was. I stared back at her, hoping any residual hostility inbred in our relationship wasn't written on my face.

She stood up straight and spoke. "Last year, I pulled over a drunk driver. It was a routine bust after a traffic violation. Officer Clark was my partner at the time, but he had a cold, so I played lead and handled everything."

"If it was routine, what was the problem?"

"There shouldn't have been a problem. But I saw a gun jutting out from under the passenger seat of the driver's car. That changed everything."

"I thought in Texas everybody had a gun."

"Concealed carry laws. If he has a weapon in the car with him, it has to remain out of view. When he stopped, it slid forward. I couldn't ignore it. The driver failed my breathalyzer test. Not by much, but enough. He claimed somebody must have hidden it in his car, but I didn't believe him."

"Did you think it was his?"

"I think someone gave it to him and he was trying to protect that person."

"Why would someone give him a gun?"

"I don't know. But the law says giving a gun to an

intoxicated person is a Misdemeanor. He wouldn't say someone gave it to him, but he said it wasn't his. I couldn't look the other way."

"What happened?"

"I took possession of the gun, and we brought the guy in. He went into lock-up while I tagged the evidence and Clark filled out the paperwork."

"Sounds pretty cut and dried."

She raised her eyebrow. "Nothing around here is cut and dried. We don't even take a case to court unless we can guarantee the district attorney that he'll win. There's too much money at stake otherwise. People get mad if they pay their taxes and bad guys end up back out on the street. Once we're sure we have a case and it goes to trial, it damn well better go our way."

"But he failed the breathalyzer test. You had the evidence. You said it was routine."

"I thought it was. The problem came when the lab pulled fingerprints off the gun and ran them through Live Scan, and the hit that came back wasn't him. It was a local lawyer who had no criminal record."

"What did he say when you brought him in? Did he give you any leads?"

"We never had a chance to ask him any questions. Clark and I went to his office to talk to him, see what we could find out. What we found was him dead in his office."

"Somebody killed him?"

"No, he killed himself." Nasty looked away. "Until that point, I thought maybe I was trying to turn it into more than it was. All I wanted was to talk to him to put my mind at ease. But without his story, the DA had to let my guy go. We had nothing to hold him except a DUI, and it was his first offense." She shook her head back and forth like it still didn't sit well with her. "I wanted to keep investigating. There had to be something there, some secret that needed to be uncovered. How else did the lawyer know we'd be coming to question him? What was he trying to hide? But the family put pressure on us to drop it. Said our actions drove their dad to suicide."

"Do you believe your actions drove him to suicide?"

"There was a note," she said. "Short and sweet: 'I didn't mean to do it.'"

"Captain Washington had you drop the case, and you quit the force."

"He did what he had to do. So did I."

I hadn't realized how long we'd been sitting alone in the lobby of the precinct. Garcia and Tex returned together. Tex's expression was suspicious. He looked back and forth between Nasty and me as if checking for bloodshed. I rolled my eyes at him.

"Captain Allen," I said. "It's late, I'm tired, and I smell. Today has been more excitement than I like. Would it be possible for the department to arrange transportation back to my house?"

"I'll take you," Nasty said. She stood up and pulled a set of keys out of her very tight jeans like a magician might make a bunch of flowers appear from inside the sleeve of his jacket. I looked away from her to Tex. I couldn't read his face. "Oh, come on, Madison. If we haven't tried to kill each other yet, we're probably safe for the ride home."

I looked back at Tex and shrugged slightly. I couldn't stop thinking about what she'd told me, about how her own actions, that seemed so by the book, had led to someone killing himself. In my own experience an action like that spoke to demons that lay under the surface of an outwardly stable person. But she was right. Any questions that remained would go unanswered.

I wrapped Rocky's leash around my wrist and followed Nasty out of the police station to her shiny silver Saab. She aimed her remote at the doors and climbed in. I dropped into the passenger seat, buckled the seatbelt, and cradled Rocky on my lap.

"Turn right," I said.

"I know where you live."

I honestly wasn't sure if that was a good thing or not.

We drove along in silence. She continued down Gaston Avenue and pulled her Saab up alongside the curb across the street from my old apartment building.

"I don't live here anymore," I said. I was delighted by the surprise I saw on Nasty's face. "Too many bad memories. No point living in the past."

She ignored my comment. "So where to? Hudson's house?"

"Thelma Johnson's house."

"Who?"

"Just drive toward Whole Foods and veer left. It's on Monticello."

She knew the area well enough to get to my street without any more directions. Once she turned, I told her to go a few blocks farther until she arrived at my address. She put the car into park.

I'd wanted to get out of the car the minute I'd first gotten into it, but I could tell Nasty had something else on her mind. Whatever weird bonding sessions we'd endured over the past few years held me in place more firmly than my seatbelt.

"Do you ever think about him?" I asked softly.

"All the time." She stared out the window as if lost in a memory. "I wish I could talk to him. Ask him why. That's all I want to know."

"You still can."

She looked at me. "You think I'm talking about Tex, don't you? Tex and I are ancient history. I'm talking about the guy who shot himself."

"You can't hold yourself responsible for what he did."

"If I could believe, and I mean really believe, that he committed suicide, then maybe I could let it go."

"He must have been hiding something. That's what you have to ask yourself: what was his secret?"

"That's what keeps me up at night." She bent down and pulled her wallet out of her handbag. She unzipped it and pulled out a small piece of coral paper. When she unfolded the paper, I saw a flat metal pin in the shape of a cross. The prayer of the guardian angel was printed on the coral paper next to where the pin had been affixed. Another smaller white piece of paper fell out and landed on her lap.

"I've carried two things with me since that day. This prayer and a copy of his note."

She handed me both. I wasn't surprised by the verse on the coral paper or the idea that a small talisman could offer her protection. Cops were like everybody else, and a belief in a higher power might have helped her do her job.

I unfolded the white piece of paper and felt my blood run cold. The suicide note was exactly as she'd told me. "I didn't mean to do it" was written in the center of the page. What other people took as a confession or an apology, I took completely differently, not because of the handwriting or the sentiment or the lack of punctuation.

But because the note was written on letterhead stationery from the legal offices of Stanley & Abbott.

TWENTY

"Why are you confiding in me?" I asked.

"Because I need your help. Tell me what you know about this case. I'm not a cop anymore. I can do things they can't."

I looked back at the paper. When Nasty had flirted with Garcia, she'd said she was investigating the murder of a local lawyer. I didn't know enough about private-sector security firms like Big Bro Security to have a reliable sense of what she may or may not have found out on her own about today's crimes. I needed to ask Tex about this so I didn't potentially damage his investigation, and I wanted to show him this note. But there was no way Nasty would allow me to keep her letter. Not without telling her why it was important to me. The person I needed to tell was Tex.

"What was the man's name?" I asked.

She took the papers from my hands and folded them back up. "Don Abbott. He was a partner at the firm of the lawyer you found today."

"And the other guy? The one you pulled over?"

She looked at me for a moment, her jawline rigid, her eyes calculating. "I don't remember."

I didn't believe that for a second.

I pointed to the papers. "Why do you carry it around with you?" She ignored me and tucked the letter and the pin back into her wallet. I waited for an answer. When she didn't say anything, I put my hand on her arm to stop her from finishing her task. "You accused me of living in the past. Wouldn't you say you're doing that yourself?"

She looked down at my hand and then up at my face. "Point taken. Now get out of my car before hell freezes over."

I didn't much mind ending my day on that note. I let Rocky do his business on the grass and then we went inside. It was late. I ate an apple on my way up the stairs and, in a reckless display of compost recycling, opened my bedroom window and dropped the core on the garden bed below. I soaked my dress in the bathroom sink, showered, and changed into my favorite yellow cotton gingham pajamas: button-front, A-line top with a white peter pan collar and matching bloomers, both trimmed with white cotton lace, and then crawled into bed.

But as tired as I'd been half an hour ago, now I was wide awake. There was no way I'd be sleeping, not after what I'd just learned from Nasty.

I threw the covers back and got back up. While I still used the landline phone at Mad for Mod, I had recently given up my home phone and relied exclusively on my cell. Which I'd left downstairs charging on the counter. I crossed the thick shag carpeting and descended the stairs. It was after ten, which I suspected was still before Tex's bedtime. I called him.

"Howdy, Night," he answered. "Thought you'd be on your way to dreamland by now."

"I would have been if you'd asked Officer Garcia to give me a ride home instead of letting Nasty do it."

"I was about to. Nobody thought Nasty was going to offer you a ride. Trust me on that."

"Well, it's a good thing she did." I dropped into one of my kitchen chairs, a recent acquisition from an estate sale. The chairs were each from different kitchen sets but matched in style. I had a walnut, a maple, and two oak. The table was birch and splintered in a couple of places. It gave me the perfect excuse to rotate through my collection of vintage tablecloths. Today the table was covered in an ivory cloth printed with colorful roosters. A collection of old milk jugs sat in the center of the table with flowers made from tissue paper and pipe cleaners that had been assembled by a class of kindergarteners. I firmly believed in supporting the preschool arts.

I pulled my earbuds out of an empty vase that sat on a shelf under the window. I lost track of what Tex said while I unwound the cord and got the buds into each ear. "Say that again?" I said.

"I said you might want to go easy on this new friendship with Nasty. She doesn't do a whole lot without a master plan."

I jumped up out of my chair and whirled around. "When are you going to learn to give me a little credit? Or, oh, I'm sorry, do you look at me and see a sad little woman who needs more friends?"

"That's not what I see when I look at you."

"Okay, then. Nasty wanted something from me. That's the only reason she'd be nice to me, right? Do we agree on that?"

"Maybe. Why?"

"Because in her attempt to get something from me, she gave me something you're not going to believe."

His voice was alert. "What's that?"

"The evidence she mixed up—the case she quit the force over? That guy was one of the partners at Stanley & Abbott law firm."

"Yeah? So?"

"You knew that already?"

"Night, when are you going to learn to give me a little credit?" he parroted back at me.

I was happy to be wearing the earbuds so I could ball up my fists properly. "What else do you know that you're not telling me?"

"A lot. And I'm not going to tell you, either. You're not

investigating this case. I am."

"Why is that, Tex? Why won't you answer that? Have you ever stopped to wonder why you're so motivated to dig into this particular case when you're the captain? You don't have to be out rattling cages. You have a desk job now. Everything you're doing is somebody else's job."

"Night, I know exactly why I'm doing what I'm doing." He was quiet for a moment. "Is that really why you called me? You got what you thought was a hot clue and wanted to pass it along?"

"I called you because I thought maybe you'd understand that I have more than a passing interest in the outcome of this case. May I remind you my friend died? All of this started when she left me that factory. I know this isn't the first time you've seen something like this. A seemingly random act that turned into something much bigger."

"What else did Nasty tell you?"

"She didn't tell me anything else. I saw Mr. Abbott's name when she showed me the note."

"What note?"

"The suicide note Don Abbott left behind."

"She had it with her?"

"She had it in her handbag with the prayer of the guardian angel."

"This is not good. Are you at Thelma Johnson's house?"

"Yes. Why?"

"I'm on my way." The call disconnected. I called back immediately. He didn't answer.

The clock told me it was a little after ten thirty, which meant it was eight thirty in California. I didn't know why the idea of Tex coming over at ten thirty at night made me feel guilty, but it did. I called Hudson.

"Hey Lady," he answered. "Kinda late for you, isn't it?"

"Once in a while I like to try something new," I said. "It's been a crazy day, and I'm off my routine."

"Crazy how? Talk to me."

"Well, like inheriting a pajama factory. I've been thinking a lot about Alice and her life, and why she gave it to me. I think she wanted me to do something with it and I don't know how to best honor her family's legacy. There's that great Sweet Dreams logo on the outside of the building."

"One thing I'm learning out here is that it takes more than a cool exterior to get interest in a business."

For a moment, thoughts of the pajama factory were replaced by Hudson's business troubles. It felt good for a moment to push my problems aside and talk about something else. Something I knew.

"You know, there's a whole community of midcentury-modern enthusiasts in Palm Springs, and I have access to them through Mad for Mod. If you want me to help generate some interest in your project through those channels, I can."

"It's not just that." In the background, I heard a girl's laugh. "Hold on," he said.

"Are you at your sister's house?"

"Yes, I'm moving to a quieter room. I appreciate the offer and just might take you up on it. Between the construction stuff and the Hollywood stuff, I'm feeling pulled in a few too many directions and I sure wouldn't mind giving one up. Why don't you take my mind off my troubles? Tell me what's going on with you."

I stretched out on the sofa, and for the next couple of minutes, it felt like a normal night with Hudson on his end of the phone and me on mine. I told him the rumors about Alice's husband and the pajama model, and about Alice's having an affair while her husband was alive. "And now, between the murder at the factory this morning and the body we found this afternoon, it feels like my whole world has gone topsy turvy."

"What murder?" he asked. "What body?" The calm tone of his voice changed.

"I told you earlier today when I called."

"When I was driving?"

"Yes. Why?"

"Your cell kept dropping out, and I only caught every third word or so. No matter. You now have my undivided attention."

I took a moment to collect my thoughts and best figure out how to explain everything that had happened. And then I heard Tex's Jeep pull up out front. "Hudson, two men were murdered, and their deaths appear to be connected to the pajama factory Alice left me. I'm cooperating with the police. They just arrived. Tex—Tex just arrived."

"It's quarter to eleven at night," Hudson said.

"I know. I was in bed, but I couldn't sleep because my mind was racing, so I called him to tell him what I'd just found out—"

"You got out of bed and called him? You didn't call me until after that, did you?"

"You talked to Nasty this morning and didn't tell me."

"That's not the same."

The conversation wasn't going the direction I'd expected. "Hudson, I called you today to talk about this. I had a meltdown at the cemetery and wanted to hear your voice."

"And?"

"And you were so calm. I told you I had just come from a murder scene."

"I told you it was a bad connection."

"That's not the point. Don't you ever get mad? Don't you ever want to just hit something? You're so calm all the time. Thirty seconds into talking to Captain Allen and I want to pull daisies out by the roots. Why is that?"

Hudson was quiet for a few beats. Finally, he spoke. "If you slow down long enough to think about what you just said to me, you'll realize you've known the answer all along." He paused for a moment. "I'm staying in California for a little bit. I love you, Lady, and I think you love me too, but not in the way we should. You want fireworks and explosions, and I want ripples in an otherwise peaceful ocean."

"You misunderstood what I said. You lived through some of your darkest days because of the case that Hollywood is interested in, and those people are turning it into a romantic comedy. Why doesn't that upset you?"

"What's really on your mind, Madison? Because I don't think it's what the Hollywood people are doing with my story."

Maybe it was the fact that he'd called it his story and not ours. Maybe it was the distance between us, both physically and emotionally. But whatever he'd said, whatever had happened, I felt we weren't in the same place and for the first time in months, I found the courage to acknowledge what terrified me the most.

"You're moving on, and I'm not. And that doesn't bother you. No matter what happens, you roll with the punches, and that makes me feel like that's it for you."

"There weren't a lot of choices for me."

"You could have fought for your life. I'm not talking about now, I'm talking about twenty years ago when you were suspected of murder. You could have fought for your innocence and maybe your whole life would have been different."

"Madison, it's taken a long time, but I've reached the end of my storm. If I seem calm about how a group of writers in a room with no windows are taking liberties with my life, it's because I know everything that happened brought me to this moment right here, right now."

"You've found inner peace and I'm just as disconnected to the world as I was when I moved to Texas."

"Then move on too," he said softly. "There's nothing keeping you in Texas. You could reopen Mad for Mod out here in Palm Springs. There's a built-in audience, just like you said. You don't have to do things the hard way and you don't have to do them by yourself. We could start over together." He was quiet for a moment. "Unless there's something keeping you in Dallas, in which case, there's not a whole lot more I can say, is there?"

"Hudson—"

"Think about this, Madison. There's only one person in your life who I've ever seen make you crazy. You say you're upset because I'm so calm. Maybe my being calm isn't the problem."

TWENTY-ONE

There was a knock on the doorframe. I didn't turn around to look. I was too stunned by what Hudson hinted at to think about rational things like letting Tex in.

"I have to go," I said. I hung up the phone and stood facing the sink, trying to get myself under control before turning around. I was feeling something, but I didn't know what. It wasn't sadness, and it wasn't anger. It took a few seconds longer than I would have liked, which probably accounted for why Tex felt like he had to knock again.

I turned slightly and spoke over my shoulder. "It's open," I said.

He tried the door. It wasn't open.

I crossed the kitchen and flipped the deadbolts. Rocky appeared at my feet and nosed his way past my legs, and past Tex's legs, into the garden. He ran over to the corner of the flower bed and peed and then ran around in circles a couple of times. That meant he wasn't done with his nightly deposit.

I pushed past Tex, descended the three concrete stairs outside, and watched Rocky. "He'll be done in a minute," I said. "It's late, and it's dark, and I won't leave him out here alone." Tex stared at me. "What?" I asked. The residual heat from my conversation with Hudson radiated off me. I knew exactly what Hudson had been getting at. It was the reason I couldn't make direct eye contact with Tex even though he was three feet away from me.

"Night, are you okay?"

"I'm fine. Why? Don't I seem fine?"

"Not really. It's fifty degrees out, and you're in your backyard in your skimpy little pajamas."

I crossed my arms over my chest. "Really? That's what you want to talk about?"

He grinned. "I'll talk about your skimpy little pajamas any time you let me. I hadn't realized we'd hit that stage of our relationship."

I looked up at his face. No way I was thinking what I was thinking. It didn't make any kind of sense. It had to be the emotional day I'd had coming to a head. The banter, the need to call Tex before I called Hudson, the crackling tension, and excitement when he made me mad. He was every single thing that was wrong with the opposite sex.

Oh my god, it was so clear.

I turned away from him and called out to Rocky. He ran back with his beanie turtle in his mouth and dropped it by Tex's feet. Tex picked it up and put it in his pocket. I scooped up Rocky, and we all went inside.

As soon as Rocky was down on the floor, I pointed to the chair. "Sit. Wait. I'm getting a robe."

"Don't do anything special on my account."

I ran upstairs and pulled a black quilted cotton robe out of the hall closet. It had three-quarter sleeves and a peter pan collar. Giant plastic buttons shaped like pansies set off a pastel paisley print in aqua, yellow, and pink. The robe had a matching quilted sleeping bonnet, and I considered wearing it to give Tex the full effect: me in all my 1960s wardrobe quirkiness.

I returned to the first floor (no sleeping bonnet) and found Tex sitting on one end of my sofa. "Well, that's no fun," he said. "I'm curious, Night, which does James prefer? The robe or the little yellow outfit underneath?"

"Leave Hudson out of this," I said. I sat down in a Milo Baughman-era gold chenille barrel chair. "We were talking about Nasty's evidence mix-up and how her suicide victim is connected to the murder from today. Something I said made you come over in the middle of the night. I want to know what it was."

"Not to be a stickler for details, but only in your world is eleven o'clock the middle of the night."

"Don't change the subject."

Tex looked out the window for a few seconds. It was unusual for me to have left the curtains open, and I figured he must have pushed them aside while I was upstairs. The streetlamp on the corner provided enough light that I could make out the top of the hedge that lined my property, but not enough to see his Jeep.

He turned away from the window and leaned forward. "You said Nasty had the note with her. That's not good. That case took place over a year ago. I knew—we all knew—she had a hard time when Don Abbott killed himself. Not all that strange for her to leave the force. Things had been difficult for her for a while for a whole bunch of reasons. But to carry that note around, that means it's still with her every day. It's driving her to act in a way she might not normally act. You've seen that kind of behavior. So have I. It's not healthy."

"But aside from the fact that Nasty should talk to the psychiatrist you keep on the police payroll, what does it have to do with me?"

"Nasty came by the police station for a reason, and I doubt it had a whole lot to do with that actress she brought with her. You two getting along, her giving you a ride home, it adds up to one thing. She wants information. What did you tell her?"

"About the case?" I thought back to earlier in the day, but so much had happened that it was cloudy in my memory. "I told her about the gun, I think. And the inheritance and the storage unit."

Tex's expression changed. "Damn it, Night."

"What? It's not a secret. And she wanted to know why you ran my prints through the database. It was pretty innocent. She said you wouldn't have done that unless you thought I was guilty or you wanted to eliminate my prints from the suspect pool, so she already knew there was something else going on."

"Then what? You two have a pillow fight?"

"What is with men and pillow fights?"

He cocked his head to the side for a moment and then said, "Nah, never mind."

I fought every instinct I had to throw a pillow at *him*. "We need to talk about this," I said.

"About what?"

"About what it means."

"What do you think it means?" he asked. He leaned forward with his forearms on his jeans, his dirty blond hair falling over his forehead. The tall turquoise and white atomic lamp in the corner threw off light that caught his ice-blue eyes.

We stared at each other. The clock ticked off seconds. It wasn't the first time I'd found myself attracted to this annoying man in front of me, but every single time it had happened, there'd been drama surrounding us. That must be what was happening right now.

I cleared my throat. "I'm talking about the case," I said.

"So am I."

"Good."

"Good."

I stood up from my barrel chair. "This is going to take a while. I'm putting on a pot of coffee."

Considering Tex's dig about my calling eleven the middle of the night, I was surprised to find him asleep on my sofa when I returned with two mugs of coffee. It wasn't the first time he'd slept there, and I had no qualms about waking him up. I held both mugs of coffee and kicked the base of the sofa with my slipper.

"Wake up," I said. "This isn't a slumber party." I held one mug out. It was yellow and had big white daisies on it.

He glared at the mug, at me, and back at the mug. "If this ever got out, I'd lose all respect."

"You know, I say the same thing every time someone sees me in public with you." I sat back down on my barrel chair. "I've been over and over this in my mind. I keep coming to the same conclusion, but it doesn't make any sense."

"What's that?"

"The murders. Something about them seems off."

Tex held his coffee mug and stared at me. "Tell me why you think that."

"The law offices were cold, right? Why? There wasn't anybody there. The cleaning woman, Frannie, said there was a note on the door of the offices telling her to go in and start working. Was she expected to find Mr. Stanley's body? She was so scared when she went into that office that I don't know if she would have called you if I hadn't been there. And she still didn't call you. I did. She said she would have no part of it and then she left."

"She didn't leave."

"She left the building, but she waited in the parking lot. She feels loyalty to the firm that employs her. I think on some level she knew staying was the right thing even though she was scared. But still, the two seem out of order."

"Maybe Mr. Sweet killed himself. Maybe he killed Mr. Stanley and then was overcome by guilt."

"You don't believe that any more than I do. We already know John Sweet was alive when my gun was put in the storage unit, and besides, there are two guns."

If I'd thought I was telling Tex something he hadn't already worked out, I knew now I was wrong. He'd already reasoned through these facts. It was my turn. "Does this timeline work? Somebody shoots Mr. Stanley and cranks the A/C to confuse the time of death. It's hot enough outside that nobody would question the fact that the air conditioner was running, at least not at first. Whoever shot Mr. Stanley gave the gun to John to hide, and John hid it in storage. If he knew about the letter from Alice, he could have just rewritten it and added the second page to get me out to Hernando's Hide-It-Away to find the gun."

"Why?"

I thought about that question. "I don't know. It was easy?"

"I don't like it. We gotta be able to show more solid motivation."

Unlike in the past when I'd floated theories to Tex and he'd quickly dismissed them, tonight we worked through details together. I didn't feel like I was being told I was wrong or to mind my own business. We were approaching the problem from different angles and maybe reaching a joint conclusion.

"Let's back up a sec," I said. "Everything seemed fine until you got a phone call when we were at Alice's house. That's when you clammed up and told me we were going to the police station and you scanned in my prints. What was that all about?"

"Confidential."

"Fine." I stood up and left the room. When I returned, I held two plastic water pistols I had left over from a Calamity Jane-themed birthday a few years back and a glass bowl of colorful sourball candies wrapped in cellophane. I set the bowl on the floor next to my feet.

"Two guns, right?" I said. Tex nodded. I set both water pistols down on the table. "Here's what I think happened. Somebody shot Mr. Stanley. One shot to the head." I set a red sourball on the table next to the gun on the left. "It happened sometime after John gave me the letter from Alice with the key. The shooter fired the gun a few more times and collected the shells, and then gave the gun to John to hide. And either because he was mad about my inheritance or simply for convenience sake, he hid it in my storage unit and made sure I discovered it. At that point, he probably sat back and waited for me to find the gun and get arrested for murder. Except I can't figure out why he'd kill himself if he thought he framed me."

"Did he know you were going to check out the box the next day?"

"No, I mean, he probably could have assumed I'd be curious, but he called me back to tell me about the memorial service. So maybe he thought I wouldn't have time to get to the storage locker."

"But you think he rewrote the letter."

"The letter was sealed, so at the time, I didn't think he knew what it said. If he's the one who wrote it, then sure, he knew. If somebody else wrote it and sealed it and tricked him, then—I don't know. That's getting awfully convoluted, especially since Alice's original letter is sitting on her dining-room table."

"That's another question. Why would her grandson leave it sitting out where you could find it?"

"I've been thinking about that," I said. "John knew I inherited the factory and the contents of Alice's house. He didn't give me keys to the house, so he probably figured I'd contact him if I wanted to do an inventory. Most times I buy out an estate, that's how I work. Even if somebody sells me the contents of their deceased parent's house sight unseen, they sometimes get emotional over one or two items, and it avoids a lot of duress if we do a walk-through together. If somebody else wrote the letter, they might not know I had an actual reason to come by and go through her belongings. Let's set that aside for the moment and keep going."

"You do know I'm not going to tell you anything about the case, right? Not that I don't appreciate the way you lay out your evidence." He used a sweeping hand to indicate my water pistol/sourball candy display.

"If you didn't want to talk about this, you wouldn't be here right now."

"Is that what you think?"

"I think you want to know what happened as badly as I do, and you know I look at things differently than cops do. Like the shell casings we found at the pajama factory. I remember looking at the condition of the factory interior. Remember I said it was like a time capsule? Aside from a lot of dirt, Sweet Dreams was pristine. It looked like it must have looked when it was operating in the fifties."

I could tell from the look on Tex's face that I'd said something of note. "That's it, isn't it?" I continued. "There were spent shell casings but no bullet holes. John Sweet was shot once. Those shells were placed there. They were from the gun that killed Mr. Stanley, weren't they? *That's* what the call was about, the call you got when we were at Alice's house. You got a hit that the shell casings at Sweet Dreams came from the gun in my storage unit."

Tex crossed his arms and leaned back against the sofa cushion. He propped his feet on my coffee table, crossed at the ankles, next to his almost empty yellow mug. "What does all that tell you?"

"John thought he was working with somebody, but that somebody double-crossed him."

"Who?"

"I don't know. Sid Krumholtz from the Truthers has been hanging around. So has Dax Fosse. Even Frannie, the cleaning woman, could be hiding something. But whoever it was framed things to look like John killed Mr. Stanley and then did a sloppy job of making it look like John killed himself. Because if John really was overcome with guilt, wouldn't he just have used the same gun? If I had waited one day to pick up that gun or get to the storage unit, the whole timeline would be different."

"Why?"

I searched my mind for something that made sense. Something that took the random bits of information and put them into a pattern. And then it clicked.

"Because now they're all dead."

"Who? The Sweet family? I don't think this is about them," Tex said.

"Not the Sweets. The lawyers. Mr. Abbott, Mr. Stanley, and John Sweet. Everybody from the law firm is dead, and now nobody knows what they were hiding."

TWENTY-TWO

I was so surprised by that sudden thought that I jumped up and started pacing. "The lawyer who killed himself—you know, from Nasty's case—he was the other partner. Mr. Abbott. John was the secretary. Mr. Abbott must have had some demons if he killed himself, right?"

"Stands to reason."

"Unless Nasty is right and somebody made it look like a suicide when it wasn't."

"Don't let Nasty's battle become yours."

"Either way, it looks like there's something about that law firm that somebody wants to keep quiet. You need to get there and find out what it is. Go through their files. Keep the place sealed and go over everything."

Tex stood up. "It's after midnight, and you need to get some sleep."

"But you said—"

"I said this is an open investigation and you're not a cop. I listened to your theories, and I'm going to check some things out. But it's late. Nothing's going to happen until tomorrow."

"Are you going to tell me what you find after you check things out?"

"Probably not, but I admire the fact that you just keep on asking." He patted me on the cheek twice and I swatted his hand away.

"What am I supposed to do now?"

"Whatever you would normally do, as long as it doesn't involve my case."

"Fine," I said. I grabbed both sides of the curtains and pulled them together, buttoning three buttons in the middle that kept them closed. "I trust you know how to lock the door on your way out."

I stormed up the stairs and ditched my quilted robe the second I was out of sight. A few seconds later, the front door closed. I watched from the side of my window as Tex left my property and climbed into his Jeep. His engine started, and he drove off. I dropped the curtains into place and crawled into bed next to Rocky.

Despite the late night, I woke naturally at five thirty. I got up and pulled on a bathing suit, and then dressed in a pair of pink floral pants and matching princess blazer, a lavender poplin shirt underneath, and pink Keds. I packed clean underwear in my swim bag along with a cap, goggles, and fresh towel. Rocky trotted downstairs with me. I opened the front door so he could do his morning routine. He ran to the tomato plant, and I stood on my front steps staring out at the street just as my Alfa Romeo pulled up in front of my hedges. Tex was behind the wheel.

As soon as the car came to a complete stop, he turned the engine off and got out. "I told you to do your regular routine. You can't do your routine without a car. Here's your car."

"My car was parked at Alice's house. Exactly how did you get it here?"

"I took your keys last night."

"*What?*"

"Technically, you gave me permission when you asked me to lock up. I believe your exact words had something to do with me knowing how to lock up on my way out. Turns out that yes, I do know how to lock up." He held out my keys and shook them. "You're welcome."

I grabbed the keys from his hand. Rocky, lighter from having fertilized the tomato plant, charged toward Tex, yapping playfully. Tex reached down and ruffled Rocky's fur. "Hey boy," he said. "All better today? You don't even remember that mean old skunk, do you?"

I'd forgotten about the skunk, about how Tex had taken Rocky and bathed him after having been sprayed. "What was in that bag you brought back to the police station last night?"

"What?"

"You brought a brown paper bag when you came back with Rocky. You set it on Garcia's desk. Nasty looked inside, but I didn't. What was it?"

"Nasty looked inside?" He grinned. I nodded. He squinted one eye against the sunlight. "It was one of my old uniforms. You smelled almost as bad as Rock, and I thought you could use a change of clothes." He assessed my pink and lavender pantsuit. "It wasn't your style."

Again, I felt what I'd felt last night. Again, I dismissed it. Like attracts like, not opposites. I knew that. I'd done favors for Tex in the past, and he'd done one for me. So what?

"How are you getting home?" I asked him.

"Uber. You should try it sometime instead of walking everywhere."

"I like walking."

"Well, there's walking, and then there's what you do, which is abusing your injured knee as a reminder of what happens when you drop your guard."

I froze where I was standing. "Where did that come from?"

He shrugged. "Therapy's given me all sorts of insights."

Before Tex's predecessor had retired, he'd employed a psychiatrist for the department and established a mandatory schedule of appointments for the precinct. Whatever it was Tex talked about during those sessions seemed to have brought him a level of peace he welcomed.

I went back inside the house. Rocky and Tex followed in that order. Once the front door was shut behind him, Tex kept talking. "Physical reminders are funny, don't you think? Look at me. I took a bullet in the butt cheek. Because of you, I seem to recall. So now every time I sit in an uncomfortable chair, I get a reminder of what happens when I look out for you."

"Did you just call me a pain in the butt?"

"A pain in *my* butt," he corrected. "I guess I did, didn't I? On that note, I'll leave before you throw something at me." He said goodbye to Rocky and left.

I knew I should have offered him a ride. I didn't. Not because I was selfish, but because in the past twenty-four hours, something had changed and it scared me. The best thing for me to do was to go to the pool and swim like I always did. My best thinking came when I was in the water.

Two hours and a full set of pruny fingertips later, I rested at the end of the lane. I'd pushed aside concerns over my personal life around the twenty-minute mark and had forced my thoughts to focus on the one thing I'd neglected since first learning of Alice's inheritance. My business.

The money from the sale of my apartment building had provided enough income to take the pressure off a dwindling client list, as had an endorsement deal with a local paint company. But the truth was, I was happiest when I was working. And just because there were no appointments on my calendar didn't mean I didn't know how to shake something loose. Richard had that crisis at The Mummy Theater, and nothing thrilled Richard like when I stepped in and took control. That's the beauty of volunteer work: there's always a project to spearhead or somebody out there dropping the ball.

I climbed out of the pool and dried off. There was minimal attendance again today. Two lanes were occupied by young competitive swimmers who were squeezing in an extra practice session. It wasn't unusual for them to show up now and then. Competitors often padded their own training with additional workouts. I recognized them by the mascots on their caps and their ragged goggle straps. I found it funny how they continually tied knots in the rubber instead of buying a new pair. What did goggles go for these days, five dollars? Surely that wouldn't break the bank.

In the shallow portion of the pool, a young instructor led a cluster of women in a water-aerobics class. Eighty- and ninety-year-old women bobbed along to "Surfin' USA." Just watching their interest in staying healthy at their age was inspirational. I carried my towel into the locker room and showered off the chlorine, and then dressed in the lavender shirt and pink flowered blazer and pants. I wasn't sure a flowered pantsuit was age-appropriate, but considering how many women ran around in yoga pants, I wasn't sure age-appropriate was even a thing anymore.

The water-aerobics class finished while I was running a comb through my hair, and soon the locker room filled with the sound of chatter. I bent down to tie my pink Keds, and when I straightened up, I was surprised to find Clara Bixby standing next to me.

Today she was dressed in street clothes, not swim gear. Her short white cap of hair was carefully styled, and her eyes were covered with large black sunglasses. Her Fire and Ice lipstick contrasted nicely with the apple green wool tunic she wore over off-white pants.

"Clara!" I exclaimed at her reflection. "I didn't think you

were here this morning."

"I wasn't. Some days I like to sleep in." She smiled. "But I did have something I wanted to show you." She pulled a photo album out of her rather large handbag and held it out. Curious, I opened the cover and saw a picture of a glamorous woman in shiny red satin pajamas. Her lipstick matched the PJs, and her bright white teeth matched the teddy bear she held cuddled under one arm. "That's Suzy," Clara said. "Wasn't she pretty?"

"Is this an ad for Sweet Dreams?"

She nodded. "It was her first ad, and it took off. It was printed in black and white in the newspapers, of course, but George was smart enough to spend the money on color film for the photo shoot. That smile, that was her trademark. She lit up the room. She was so popular back then. My sisters and I loved to watch her. Each of us married after the war ended, but it was fun to watch Suzy entertain the boys. She was just a girl when we had to get jobs to help Mamma with the bills. We all made sure Suzy didn't come to the pajama factory for a job like us. Even after she became their top model, she had to rely on me to unlock the building to let her in. I told her if I had anything to say about it, she'd never have to worry about keeping track of the key to the factory."

Below the ad of Suzy was a black and white newspaper clipping that showed three people. I immediately recognized Suzy on the left and a younger Clara in the middle.

"Who is that man?" I asked.

She turned the scrapbook toward her. "That's my first husband."

I tried to get another view from my upside-down angle. "He looks familiar."

"That's Vernon for you. He just has one of those faces."

My head snapped up at the mention of the man in the picture's name. "Did you say Vernon?"

"Yes. Why?"

Vernon was the name of the man who had given Alice the Valentine's Day card she'd been using to mark her page in the library book on her nightstand. Possibly the other love of her life that she'd hinted at in her posthumous letter. How many Vernons could there be?

"Clara, I'm very sure I've seen him before. Is that possible?"

"You probably saw his picture on the news recently. I always used to tell him his job would be the death of him, and sure enough, he was shot at work, right in his law office."

"He was a lawyer?"

"Yes. Vernon was the Stanley in Stanley & Abbott."

TWENTY-THREE

Mr. Stanley was Vernon. Vernon had been Alice's secret companion. Alice's grandson worked at Vernon's law firm, and both Vernon Stanley and John Sweet had been killed a day after they'd informed me of my inheritance of the pajama factory where Mr. Stanley's first wife's sister had died. It was like *Days of our Lives,* senior edition.

And it was one more thing that brought me back to the law firm.

Clara stared at the photo. "The photographer liked how we looked, all standing together like that. Vernon was a doll, but we were not without our share of problems," she continued.

"I'm sorry to hear that," I said. "Relationships aren't easy."

Her face softened slightly. "Things became difficult after Suzy's death."

"You said he was your first husband. I hope—I mean, not to be forward, but—"

"There were three. I gave up after that and became a Bixby again. Sometimes a woman needs to carry her own mantle."

I nodded, though I was only half paying attention. Tex had warned me off his case, but Clara Bixby and her possibly philandering husband, who may or may not have been the love of Alice Sweet's life, was a whole other distraction. And truthfully, it was a welcome one. Clara looked at me like she regretted showing me her scrapbook. She took it from my hands and folded it shut.

"Clara, would you like to get a cup of coffee?" I asked.

"Oh, no, dear. I'm headed out of town this afternoon and need time to get home and pack."

"Going anywhere interesting?"

She smiled. "Sometimes I like to just fade away while no one is looking." She put the scrapbook in her straw tote bag, paused for a moment, and then pulled it back out. "Fiddlesticks. This scrapbook isn't doing any good collecting dust in my linen closet. I know you have an interest in the pajama factory. Why don't you borrow it? But be a dear, and please do return it when you're done." She tapped the cover. "Lots of memories in there."

"Of course. Thank you." I tucked the scrapbook into my bag and finished applying lip tint while she left. Her scrapbook would be fun to look at and maybe even provide inspiration for a future job. At least that's what I told myself.

I collected Rocky from the doggie station and drove to Mad for Mod. While I navigated traffic, I thought about what I'd learned from Clara. Alice's request to have her grandson execute her will made sense now. In the time I'd known Alice, I'd learned she was a bright woman who didn't discount the possibility of romance regardless of her age. As recently as a few years ago she'd accepted a date with a man from the pool. But if she and Vernon had a relationship in the past that she'd cherished, I could imagine her wanting to see him one last time.

Mr. Stanley had been surprised when I told him John had called me to execute Alice's will. I remembered the blush creeping up over his cheeks when I'd mentioned her name. I'd interpreted his surprise being because they weren't in the business of estate planning. But was it because he'd been surprised by the mention of Alice? If they'd been as close as I was starting to think, would he have recognized her name?

Clara's scrapbook indicated that Vernon was familiar with Sweet Dreams. Is that where he and Alice had met? And after the accident, when George withdrew and went out on the road as a traveling salesman, did Mr. Stanley strike up a friendship with Alice that had become something more?

Everything seemed to be intertwined. Including John Sweet's employment at Stanley & Abbott. Had he known about Alice and Mr. Stanley's past relationship? Or had Alice suggested John seek employment there so she could maintain a private connection to the man she loved? I didn't claim to know. I'd thought I knew Alice, but I'd learned so much more about her since her passing than I'd ever expected. Not for the first time, I wished she were here so I could talk to her about her life. But death was final. I could still talk to Alice, but from here on out, it would be a one-sided conversation.

It felt good to be back in my office, alone. I pulled up my email and read the most recent one from Richard, which turned out to be a simple CALL ME. It was early enough that calling Richard would likely wake him up. So, with glee, I did. He answered before the first ring ended.

"Madison, great. I was hoping you'd call. Look, I don't want to tell you how to hire staff, but your new assistant is a little green, and maybe you shouldn't delegate projects like this—"

"Richard, slow down." He stopped talking. "Connie is helping me out temporarily. Everything is under control."

"You better not be saying that to make me feel better."

"Tell you what. Let me iron out a few more details, and I'll come to your office. If not today, then tomorrow. Okay?"

"I'm counting on you, Madison."

I hung up the phone and doodled hearts along the side of my sheet of notes. It seemed I was dealing with some unfortunate timing of my own. Richard had been pushing me to have the conclave at the pajama factory all along. Under normal circumstances, it might have even been a good idea. But now, the very same location that should have been mine for the taking was a crime scene, and I didn't know when Tex was going to let me back in. I could call him, but he had more important things on his agenda than my need to organize a party.

Tex may have been doing a nice thing by retrieving my car from Alice's house, but there also remained the possibility that he was trying to eliminate any reasons for me to spend time there. But his investigation surrounded the law firm of Stanley & Abbott, not Alice. The two had gotten linked in my mind, but I could just as easily reason that John Sweet had simply taken advantage of me. Truthfully, it didn't even matter that Tex had asked me to mind my own business. I didn't want to be involved in his homicide. I wanted a distraction, and Richard's crisis had delivered one.

I drove to Alice's house and let myself in with the spare set of keys I still had. The interior of the house was as I'd left it. I shut and locked the front door and let Rocky run through the house while I went down the hall. The last time I'd been here, I'd gone directly to the kitchen and had gotten distracted by the copy of the letter on the table and the handwriting mismatch. Any other exploration had been postponed. But this wasn't a crime scene. I could stay here as long as I wanted—especially since the inheritor of the house was now deceased. Assuming there were no other family members named in the will, the house, already paid for, would eventually fall into the hands of the bank. It would be months before an appraiser came through here. And the contents belonged to me, so I'd have to do this sooner or later.

I didn't need months. A couple of hours would probably do it. And the first place I went was Alice's bedroom. It was a hunch, nothing more, but I'd been through enough closets of women of a certain age to know somewhere along the course of their lives, they'd learned to keep their private and personal papers hidden on the top shelf behind the hatboxes.

The kitchen table was as I'd left it: Alice's correspondence scattered across the surface. I set my bag on top, and it tipped over from the imbalance of Clara's scrapbook inside. I pulled the scrapbook out and laid it on top of the stationery, tossed my keys into my handbag, and went to the bedroom to see what I could find.

I shifted a tier of hatboxes and two clear zippered comforter bags out of the way and found what I was looking for: a cognac leather train case stuffed with correspondence like the letters on Alice's table.

I could have written a handbook.

I eased the train case off the shelf and set it down on the carpet and then lowered myself to the floor and flipped the case open. It was so full that it hadn't closed properly. I pulled out a stack of photos dated from 1972 and flipped through them until I found a bunch with Alice and the man I now knew to be Vernon Stanley. I quickly determined that their relationship wasn't short lived. Changing hairstyles and fashions indicated their romance had spanned several years, maybe even a decade. Throughout the photos, Alice's smile never wavered. It was obvious her time with him made her happy. Yet I wondered: how had she felt about the fact that he'd been married? Or that she had been too?

I corralled the photos back into a pile and returned them to the train case. I set the case on the corner of the bed and was about to explore the closet in the spare bedroom when Rocky barked. This wasn't his normal I-Found-A-Toy bark or his I-Have-To-Poop bark. This bark said Something's Wrong.

I went to the hall bathroom and pushed aside the curtains. There was a second car in the driveway parking me in. There was absolutely no reason for me to be nervous about my presence in Alice's house. It would be easy to verify that, as the inheritor of the contents of the house, I had the right to come and go as I wished. But when two police squad cars turned onto the street and glided to a halt alongside the front edge of the property, I knew this had nothing to do with my inheritance.

I called to Rocky and shushed him. "Be a good dog and go into the bedroom. I'll take care of this. I'll be right back, I promise." I kissed him and gave him a push toward the bedroom just as a key turned in the front door. The door swung open and any fear I had turned to confusion when Erin, the indie actress from California, stepped inside.

"Madison?" she said. She flung her long, highlighted hair over her shoulder. "You're the intruder?"

"I'm not intruding. What are you doing here? Where did you get a key?"

"My grandmother sent it to me before she died." She looked as confused as I felt.

"Your grandmother?" I asked.

"Yes. Didn't I tell you? My grandmother was Alice Sweet."

TWENTY-FOUR

"You're related to Alice?" I asked.

"Sure, well, sort of. Alice was married to my grandfather before he died," she said. "That's how I first found out about you. She told me what happened. When she died, I thought it was a sign. You know, the audition in Hollywood, her being your friend, like the universe was talking to me."

"Through the death of your sort-of grandmother," I said in a tone that may have suggested I didn't believe her.

She shrugged. "I've been consulting with an astrophysicist, and she says there are messages all around us. We just have to listen for them. I've been meditating every night and opening myself up as a portal for deeper communication with spirits, and that's what led me here."

If I didn't know Erin was related to Alice, then I wondered who else didn't. "Has anyone from the local police department contacted you recently?"

"Not since the other night when we were at the police station. Why would they? Besides, nobody knows I'm here except for the hotel staff. Not even my agent. Or my brother. I wanted to fly completely under the radar on this trip, so it didn't leak out later that I knew about the role in the movie or had time to prepare."

"But you told me your agent was the one who told you about the part, right?"

She looked embarrassed. "He's not really my agent. I mean,

he's an agent, but he's not mine—at least not yet. He's my boss. I mostly answer the phones in his office and schedule lunches for him. And he doesn't know he told me. I was outside his office, and I overheard him talking on the phone."

"Your name—why isn't your last name Sweet?"

"I changed it when I moved to Hollywood. Got a little closer to the front of the alphabet, which helps when it comes to auditions. Haney was my mom's maiden name, so it still feels like me."

I wanted to put my arms around Erin and console her, but there was so much more to that consolation than she knew. Not only had Alice died, but now her older brother, John, had too, and his death had been more violent and less expected. It would be up to the police department to notify the families of the deceased, not me. And while I'd been able to build up enough plausible deniability to explain that my impulse to come here wasn't related to Tex's case, I knew as soon as I told Erin about her brother's murder, I'd be stepping on the toes of Tex's investigation. Heck, I'd be squashing it like a bug under the rubber soles of my pink canvas sneakers.

Two police officers arrived. They got out of their vehicle and approached the house. They remained a few feet back from where Erin stood. I looked from one to the other. Neither one was familiar. "Are you with the Lakewood Police Department?" I asked.

"No. Dallas PD."

"Okay," I said. "I'm Madison Night. There's been some confusion here. I didn't break into this property." I held up the keys. "I inherited the contents when the owner died."

"My grandma gave you her house?" Erin asked.

"No, not the house. She gave me what was inside the house. John said he inherited the actual building." I looked at the officers. "I think this was a big mix-up."

The lead officer stepped forward and addressed Erin. "Ms. Haney, do you want to press charges against this woman for being on your property?"

"Me? No, she's right," she said. "I don't even know if it is my property. It was Grandma's house so I thought she would have left it to one of us, but I won't know the truth until I talk to my brother."

"You haven't talked to John since you've been here?" I asked Erin.

"No. Like I said, I didn't tell anybody I was coming. Our family wasn't all that close, and nobody knew I'd been back in touch with Grandma."

I turned back toward the officer in charge and glanced at his nameplate. "Officer Lopez, can I talk to you for a moment?"

He looked at Erin and then at the other officer. "Stay with her," he said to his partner. He looked at me and tipped his head backward, indicating the porch.

About a minute later we were standing on the front stoop. "Officer, I have no idea what the protocol is in a situation like this. That lady's brother inherited this house, but he was murdered yesterday. I don't think she knows. I don't even know if his identity has been released to the press. Captain Allen at the Lakewood Police Department is in charge of the investigation."

"Captain? Why is the captain in charge? Should go to the first officer on the scene."

"He was the first officer on the scene." I waved my hand back and forth. "I probably shouldn't be telling you any of this, but I don't know what else to do. Can't you call the LPD and confirm what I'm saying with them?"

"We're not in Lakewood. This call goes to our precinct, and I'm going to have to write up a report."

"Fine," I said. "But you could save a lot of effort if you'd just call Captain Allen."

"What did you say your name was?"

"Madison Night."

It was hard to tell when my name would mean something and when it wouldn't. I'd started paying cash at the Whole Foods so the checkout ladies would stop offering commentary about my life. Even Paintin' Place, the paint store where I'd named and endorsed a line of mid-century inspired paints, had become a tricky location. The owner kept asking me to write a column called "Ask Madison." It had nothing to do with Mad for Mod and everything to do with my low-level notoriety, which remained the number-one reason I kept turning down the opportunity.

But today, nothing. If Officer Lopez knew who I was, he had a heck of a poker face. I stood on the porch while he made a series of calls that led to the exact outcome I'd expected.

He held out his phone to me. "Captain Allen wants to talk to you."

I took the phone. "Hello?" I said.

"What did I tell you, Night?" he said.

"Hi, Captain Allen," I said politely. "I'm standing here with Officer Lopez from the Dallas Police Department. He was called out to the house of Alice Sweet by her granddaughter, Erin Haney—you know her as the actress who you met yesterday, the one who is working with former police officer Donna Nast, remember?—she said she saw my car parked here overnight, and then when it was back today, she got suspicious and called the local police."

Tex cursed, reaching the same unavoidable conclusion that I had. That on top of everything else, he bore the responsibility of delivering the news of Erin's brother's death. "Erin didn't leave word with anyone in California that she was coming here, so you probably haven't been able to reach her. I've already told Officer Lopez about the situation, but I would think you'd like to talk to her yourself, all things considered."

"Keep your mouth shut until I get there, Night."

"Great. I'll see you soon." I handed Lopez's phone back to him and smiled. "He's going to join us."

"I heard."

By the time Tex arrived, it felt like a veritable party. Two officers, Erin, and a couple of neighbors who came over to check out what was happening before returning with coffee and cookies. The officers had felt it best to keep me out of the house until my presence had been verified in some official capacity. Figured I'd need Tex for that.

He was dressed in a suit and tie like the day he'd met me at the pajama factory for the walkthrough. Every time I saw Tex dressed this way, I felt like I was in a parallel universe where I was still me but everybody around me was slightly off.

I felt Tex's glare from under his mirrored sunglasses and stood out of the way. He turned toward the officers, and the three of them spoke. One of the neighbors interrupted and handed him the last mug of coffee. He held up his hand in refusal but a few seconds later called her back and took it. I couldn't help noticing he appeared much more at ease with the plain black mug than the one with yellow daisies from last night.

This was stupid. I was standing by myself on the front lawn and Erin was inside all alone. The woman was about to get some very bad news, and even though I wasn't related to her in any way, I was arguably less of a stranger than the police who were ignoring her. I went past them into the house. Lopez put his hand out and I looked at him, then at Tex, then back at him. "I'm going inside to sit with Erin. I trust you all understand why it seems important to me that she's not alone right now."

Lopez looked at Tex, who nodded. I went inside and sat next to Erin at the kitchen table. She had Clara Bixby's scrapbook open on top of the pile of paper that had been sitting on the table and was flipping through it. "Was this Grandma's?" she asked.

"No, that belonged to one of the ladies who worked at Sweet Dreams," I said. "She loaned it to me." I flipped to the first page and tapped my finger on the photo of Clara and Suzy. "That's her," I said. "Her sister was a model, but I think they all look glamorous, don't you?"

"Yes," she said. "God, I bet the costume designers in Hollywood love stuff like this. It's from that time. So much easier to get the look right when you have something to copy."

I was startled by what she'd said. "That's what I do. In decorating. You came to my studio the other day, remember? I specialize in mid-century design and I study old movies to get the style right. Doris Day movies are my favorite."

"I know," she said, and then shrugged. "Or at least I know what the writers put in their character sketch about you."

She flipped through the scrapbook, and we took turns pointing out stylistic details that dated the photos. The front door opened, and Tex walked in. He'd taken his sunglasses off and his demeanor had changed.

"Ms. Night, can you give me a moment with Ms. Haney?" he asked.

"Sure. I'm—I'll—" I glanced at the table. Clara's scrapbook was open on top of Alice's correspondence. Once Tex broke the news to Erin, I didn't think she'd notice the mess in front of her, but I didn't like the idea of leaving everything laid out like that.

Tex seemed to follow my thoughts. "Ms. Haney," he said, "can I speak to you in the living room?"

"Sure," she said. She stood up and left the room. Tex followed.

I closed the scrapbook. Alice's stationery, stamps, and address book were still sitting out. I could have swept them into a bag and tossed them into a closet, but out of respect for Alice's otherwise tidy nature, I collected them into a neat stack and then carried it to the bedroom. A small ivory envelope lined in aqua fell and fluttered to the carpet in the hallway. I balanced the stack on my left hip and bent down to pick up the envelope. When I saw the handwriting on the outside, I dropped the rest of the papers on the floor.

The handwriting matched that on the sealed letter I'd been given by John Sweet. I flipped the envelope over and checked the return address.

Erin Haney, Hollywood, California.

TWENTY-FIVE

I tore my stare away from the pages. "Erin?" I called. She turned around and looked back at me. I held up the envelope. "Is this your handwriting?"

She stepped away from Tex and came over to me. My mind raced, trying to come up with a plausible reason for asking the question. She took the envelope and stared down at it, slowly running her fingertips back and forth over the letters. "No, that's how my brother writes. Grandma and I wrote to each other, but her handwriting was hard to read. John told me she used to ask him to write stuff for her when the shaking got bad." She held the envelope back toward me. "I don't know why he would have written my return address on an envelope, though. He probably meant to address it to me and made a mistake."

I took the envelope from her and ran the creased edge under my thumb and forefingers. "That makes sense," I said. I stared at the address for a moment and then set it on the table and looked at her. "Alice must have enjoyed writing to you. I'm glad you were able to make a connection before she passed away."

Erin smiled sadly. Behind her, Tex stood in the hallway watching us. His expression was hard to read. The news he had to give wasn't the type anybody would enjoy delivering and my holding up Erin simply prolonged the difficulties of his task. "Sorry for the interruption. Captain Allen is waiting for you," I said.

Erin turned and looked at Tex, and then back at me. "Thanks, Madison, for everything. I like knowing Grandma had a friend like you."

Erin walked toward Tex, and the two of them continued until they were out of my line of vision. I looked at the envelope again. The same neat letters that looked like they'd been written on top of an imaginary ruler line looked back at me.

I scooped up the pile of papers that I'd dropped and let myself into the bedroom. Rocky sat on the floor chewing the pompom trim of the coverlet on Alice's bed. The coverlet was slightly askew. I set the papers on the bed and sat next to them. Rocky jumped up and stuck his nose under the pile.

I stuffed Alice's train case of photos into the bottom of my tote bag and set Clara's scrapbook on top. "Ready to get out of here, Rocky?" I said. Rocky jumped down from the bed and stood in front of the door. I pulled his leash out of my pocket and clipped it onto his collar, and then opened the door. He led me back down the hallway to the living room.

Tex stood with his arm around Erin's shoulders. Her eyes were red, and despite her apparent attempts not to cry, her chest heaved sporadically with ragged breaths. She looked at me and then back at the ground. I looked at Tex, who tilted his head toward the front door. I tightened my grip on Rocky's leash and went outside. Based on what I'd learned about Erin's relation to Alice, which in turn indicated her relationship to John, I suspected Tex was going to accuse me of knowing more than I did. And if I was going to be accused of something, it wasn't going to be ignorance.

Rocky ran toward the officers who stood in the yard. Lopez looked down at him for a moment but then resumed his conversation with his partner. What kind of a person ignores a Shih Tzu?

Disgusted, I tugged Rocky's leash and headed toward my

car. Erin's rental had parked me in. I glanced at the house and saw Tex and Erin walk out. He said something to her and then jogged over to me.

"Where do you think you're going?" he asked.

"I'm leaving."

"What's in the bag?"

"Pictures. Scrapbook. Reference material."

"Reference material," he repeated. He looked into the bag, and because I was in a generous mood, I held the handles open a little to make it easier for him.

"This is not a crime scene. You already know I inherited the contents of this house. These photos were inside a closet in the bedroom. Is there a problem with any of that?"

"Nope. Knock yourself out. Do you want to take anything else? Need help carrying an armoire?"

"Not today." I looked past him at Erin. She was standing alone a few feet from the Dallas PD. "How'd that go?"

"About as expected. It doesn't seem like the family was very close, but I think she might be in shock."

I reached into my tote bag and pulled out the aqua-lined envelope. "I found this while I was cleaning up. I'd be willing to bet it's the same handwriting from the letter John Sweet gave me."

He took the envelope, stared at the front, and then flipped it over like I had. "That's the actress," he said, surprised.

"I know. Didn't you hear me ask her about it?"

"No. A call came in after you pulled her aside. Why would she forge her grandmother's letter to you?"

"I don't know. I asked her about it, and she said it's John's handwriting. She said Alice's handwriting had gotten bad, and John sometimes rewrote things for her, which could be true. It still seems a little weird since this looks like it came *from* her, not *to* her."

"No stamp," Tex said.

I hadn't noticed that. "Maybe she's right about John making a mistake."

"And if she lied?"

"If she's lying, then she also lied about not knowing about my inheritance. She would have had to know if she copied the letter to me."

He held the envelope up. "Can I keep this?"

"You're asking me?"

"Everything in that house is yours, right? Technically, I need your permission."

"Will you tell me what she said?"

"Not necessarily," he said.

I sighed. "Knock yourself out."

Erin moved her car to let me out of the driveway. As I drove away from Merriman Park, I checked in with Connie, who assured me that, aside from a cranky mother/daughter team who couldn't decide on a bedroom set, things at Mad for Mod were under control. That was the good news. The bad news was that Richard was still having fits over the status of the theater manager meeting. I could have handled him via email or phone, but that hadn't worked so far. I'd been forcing my routine for weeks, and I couldn't shake myself out of my rut. I drove to The Mummy to deal with him in person.

The Mummy Theater was parked in a strip mall called Casa Linda Plaza on the eastern side of Lakewood bordering Garland. The theater had changed hands several times over the years before being bought by a group of investors who wanted to show classic movies on the big screen. As the world changed and the movie-going public grew younger, it became increasingly difficult to fill the seats, which had a direct impact on Richard's job as the theater manager and head of the Classic Movie Club he'd formed. Good thing he had an unpaid staff of volunteers on which to take out his stress.

I parked in front of the theater and let myself in. The Mummy operated on Friday and Saturday nights, along with the occasional Sunday matinee, so the other days of the week were considered "office hours." Rocky and I walked past the empty concession stand, through the door behind a wall of heavy black curtains, behind the poster for *Cool Hand Luke*, and up the stairs.

Richard wasn't alone. He sat at his desk, and Dax Fosse from the Historical Preservation Society sat across from him. The air smelled vaguely sweet, and a stick of incense burned from a wooden fixture on the corner of Richard's desk. Even before I assessed the smile on Richard's face, I knew he'd reverted to his favorite way of taking the edge off his stress.

"Hey, there, Madison," Richard said. "Dax, this is Madison. You know Madison. Hey, Madison. Remember Dax?"

"Hi, Richard, hi, Dax," I said. I looped Rocky's leash over the doorknob and opened the window. "You boys look like you could use some fresh air," I said.

"Hey, yeah, good idea," Richard said. Dax merely sat in the chair with his eyes narrowed and a goofy smile on his face. "To what do we owe the pleasure?"

"Connie said you had concerns over the status of the weekend's agenda."

Dax narrowed his eyes. "You could have called."

"You are right. I could have called." I switched on a small fan and then leaned back against the bookcase by the window and waved my hand back and forth to encourage the circulation of air. "But what would be the fun in that?"

"Yeah, man, Madison's all about fun. You are a fun girl. Woman. Lady. You. Are. A. Fun. Lady. I was just telling Dax how much fun you are."

"Really?" I crossed my arms in front of my floral cotton blazer. "Dax, it seems that you and I didn't get off on the right foot the day we met. Or, come to think of it, the time we met after that."

"No worries, Fun Lady Madison," he said. He looked at Richard and held out a fist. Richard made a fist too, and they bumped knuckles.

"So, Richard, do you think you can put the brakes on the *Pineapple Express* long enough for me to give you a status report?"

The two men laughed like that was the funniest thing they'd heard in the past fifteen minutes. Perhaps longer, but honestly, I suspected they didn't have a solid grasp on the concept of time.

"Dude. I mean Lady. Hey, that's funny. Dude Lady Madison. Speaketh." Again with the laughter. I swear, when this weekend was over I was searching this place for Richard's stash and flushing it.

I opened the tray on the printer and pulled out a few sheets of paper, and then picked up a pen from Richard's desk. "Write this down," I said.

"You write it down."

"I want it to be in your handwriting, so there is no question that you wrote it."

"Fine," he said. He uncapped the pen and poised it over the paper. "Go."

I dictated what I'd lined up so far: pick the theater managers up at their hotel, shuttle them to White Rock Lake for an informal afternoon picnic. Shuttle them to The Mummy for cocktails and a late-night showing of *The Pajama Game*. The movie would end around eleven, and the theater managers could go back to their hotel or stick around and explore the building. I knew from Richard's stories that the general managers had a near-obsession with how they ran their theaters and often the conclaves ran well into the following morning.

"Hey, you should switch those," Dax said. "Show the movie then go to the pajama factory."

"Nobody's going to the pajama factory. The meeting always ends with a late-night showing of a movie. That's tradition," I said.

"Shake things up, man. Be cray," Dax said.

"Cray?" I repeated.

"Crazy. I lost my Z." He looked from me to Richard, who had drawn a line through "pajama game" and written "pajama party" underneath. Dax reached across the desk and slapped his hand on the paper. "Did you hear me, man? I lost my Z."

"Gotta get your Zs, man. Can't live without Zs."

"I'm Dax. With an X. I got an X but no Z."

These guys were toasted! I was a little concerned about what would happen to my own mental state if I stayed, not to mention Rocky's. I took a red marker from the cocktail shaker that Richard used to hold pens and wrote CALL MADISON across the sheet of paper.

I picked up the phone and called Hunan Palace, a Chinese takeout restaurant nearby that I frequented on occasion. "I'd like to place an order for delivery to The Mummy theater. Give me two orders of chicken wings, two orders of char siu pork, and half a dozen eggrolls." I started to recite my credit card number but realized I hadn't eaten regularly over the past few days. "Add an order of shrimp fried rice and keep one of those eggrolls with it. I'll pick it up myself and pay for the order when I arrive. Tell your delivery person they're going to have to knock a long time before the door is answered," I finished.

"Knock three times," Richard said.

"Knock on wood," Dax said.

"Knockwurst. Knockwurst. Knockwurst. Say knockwurst,"

Richard said.

I hung up the phone. There was no way I was going through this again tomorrow. I picked up Richard's notes and ran a copy off on the printer and then set the original back on his desk. "Richard, Dax, it's been a pleasure. Hunan Palace is bringing you food. Eat it. Do not mess with my agenda. Got it?" I folded the copy and slid it into my handbag.

"Sure, Dude Lady Madison," Richard said as I left the room.

I walked to Hunan Palace, paid the tab, and picked up my food. When I returned to the car, Dax was on the sidewalk in front of the theater.

"Madison, wait up." He jogged over toward me. His second-hand blazer flapped open, displaying a T-shirt with the movie poster from *The Warriors* on the front. There was a time when that might have made a statement, but considering I'd recently seen the same shirt at a trendy store in the Northpark Mall, the only statement it made was "I overpaid for this T-shirt."

I set my takeout on the center console and stood back up. "What's up?"

"Here," he said. He pulled two twenties out of his wallet and held them out. "For the takeout. You don't need to pay for our food."

I put my hands up in front of me. "My treat." I pointed toward the restaurant. "But if you go in and pick it up, you'll save yourself the tip money."

Dax didn't move. I got the feeling his offer to pay for the food wasn't all about paying for the food.

After an awkward length of time, I said, "I need to be going."

"Hold up. Have you made a decision yet? About what you're going to do with the building downtown?"

"No," I said honestly. "I have some ideas, and you can rest assured I'm not interested in tearing down the building or selling it to a developer. But there are more issues for me to consider here than applying for historical status."

"Why are you fighting me on this?" Dax asked.

"There's no fight. I'm not in a rush to decide the fate of the building, and I want to feel good about whatever I decide."

He jabbed at the air between us with a pointed finger. "You can drag your feet all you want, but know this. I'll find a way to get inside that building whether you give me access or not."

TWENTY-SIX

I straightened up, surprised by Dax's outburst. He had never mentioned a desire to get inside Sweet Dreams. So far, the only thing he'd wanted was for me to acquire historical designation for the factory. His motivation, which at first was to protect a historically significant building, now came from a completely different place than a love of the past. "I thought you wanted to protect the building. Why do you want to get inside so badly? What do you think you're going to find?"

Dax seemed to have lost some of his bravado. "Being responsible for getting a building like Sweet Dreams on the historical register is a big deal. We'll get national attention for the HPSD."

"Are you sure that's all you're looking for?" I stood my ground. Whether my confidence came from the pink floral pantsuit or the fact that I was easily six inches taller than he was, I felt in control. "I think you should pick up your food and go back upstairs to Richard," I said. "I have a lot to get done today."

I climbed into my car. Dax stood on the sidewalk outside The Mummy while I backed out of my space. The vision of his narrowed eyes staring at me long after I pulled out of the parking lot eroded my confidence as I drove away.

Adrenaline I hadn't been aware of now coursed through my arms and legs. It took half a mile for me to calm down. There was no reason for me to be upset by what he'd said, except that something about Dax Fosse seemed off. It took a moment to realize what it was: there'd been no signs of the stoner dude once he left Richard's office. Did that mean what I'd seen in The Mummy had been an act? And if so, what was behind it?

Ever since I'd learned of my inheritance, I'd been surrounded by people who had an interest in Sweet Dreams for their own purposes. Dax had been on that list. His motivation had seemed innocent enough, if a little on the high-pressure side. But this confrontation, right now, was about something completely different. Dax Fosse didn't care about getting historical designation for the building. He wanted to get in just like everybody else.

I pulled into a grocery-store parking lot and called Tex.

"Where are you?" he said.

I glanced at the takeout bag from Hunan Palace. "Getting lunch." I paused. I only knew about Hunan Palace because of Tex. "I just had a run-in with that little guy from the Historical Preservation Society, Dax Fosse. Do you remember him? He was at the pajama factory the day we walked through?'

"What did he want?"

"That's the thing. Dax and Richard Goode were in Richard's office at The Mummy, and they were—they appeared to be—"

"Let me guess. They were baked."

"Yes. At least I thought so when I was there. But then Dax came after me, and it is my very strong feeling that he might have been faking it."

"Faking it," Tex repeated.

"Yes. Pretending to be stoned when he wasn't. He didn't exactly threaten me, but—I don't know. I don't think his interests are isolated to me registering the building for historical status."

I expected Tex to tell me I imagined it or to ask me more questions about Dax. Something. Instead, he asked, "Did you agree to use your pajama factory for a charity event this weekend?"

"No. I very specifically did *not* agree to that. Why?"

"There are picketers at the pajama factory. They said something about an event. We're out there doing our final walkthrough before I try to contact the owner to release the crime scene." He paused to make sure I caught his emphasis on the words contact the owner. "If we release it now, the place is going to be swimming with thrill seekers and lookie lous. Not my dream situation."

"Not mine either," I said. "Who else knows you did that walkthrough?"

"Everybody, now. There's a news van parked across the street."

"I'm even more suspicious of Dax now. He was there when I went over the agenda for the charity event with Richard and, trust me, that plan did not involve Sweet Dreams. Are you going to look into his background? See if he has any unexpected ties to our case?"

"My case."

"Whatever."

"I'm checking out a different lead. Garcia and Sirokin are there. It wouldn't hurt for you to get there too."

Tex's news didn't change the fact that I was hungry. I called Connie first and asked her to get on the internet and find out everything she could about the picketing at the factory and then call me back. My fried rice could be reheated, but the eggroll had an expiration date. I ate it in the car on my way to Deep Ellum and wiped my hands on the poor excuse for a napkin they'd provided. When I arrived at Sweet Dreams, I pulled up behind the same white news van that had been there the day Tex and I did our walkthrough and got out.

A small crowd of people stood on the sidewalk facing the

building. Sid and his team of protestors were in front of the doors that had been held shut with a heavy chain. Tex hadn't rethreaded the chain after we'd left, but the doors were locked and yellow crime-scene tape had sealed them from reentry. I sidled up behind the crowd and leaned in to get a closer look at the situation.

"Somebody was murdered in that building," said a woman on the edge of the crowd. "I thought it would be hip to live downtown, but not if that's the kind of neighbors I'll have."

My phone vibrated in my hand and I answered. The surrounding noise made it difficult to hear, though the display told me it was Connie. I stuck a hand over one ear and pressed the phone against the other. "Did you find anything out?"

"Yes, and you're not going to like it."

I stepped away from the crowd so I could hear her better. "Talk to me," I said.

"Well, it turns out a family member is suing you for ownership of the pajama factory. Something about you making up the entire story about inheriting it and not having anything to back up your claims."

"What family member?" I asked, although as far as I knew, there was only one person left who could protest my ownership.

"It says here a Sid Krumholtz."

Relief settled in on me. "Sid is the head of the Truthers. His organization sleuths for the truth. Their whole goal is to get inside and look for evidence in a very old case about a model who died in the factory. There's no family relationship there."

"All that might be true, but it doesn't change what I found out. When the Supreme Court passed the same-sex marriage laws in 2015, he was one of the couples who got married that day."

"Who did he marry?" I asked, already dreading the answer.

"The grandson of your friend. He married John Sweet."

TWENTY-SEVEN

I looked back up at the door to Sweet Dreams and spotted Sid Krumholtz glaring back at me from under a picket sign. "Sid and John. Sid and John?"

"That's what it says here. Sid is suing you for a property grab. You didn't know?"

I thought back to Frannie, the cleaning lady at the law firm, who had told me about John's lawsuit against Stanley & Abbott when Mr. Stanley made an inappropriate comment about John's sexual orientation. What had she said? *He started here as the secretary, but if Mr. Stanley or Mr. Abbott did one thing wrong, John probably could have owned the firm.*

I looked at Sid again. He held his picket sign proudly over his head and paraded back and forth across the façade of the pajama factory. If he and John had been married, then John could have told him about my inheritance. Sid had been trying to get in all along—or trying to keep me out. He could have gotten the keys from John when he wasn't looking. He had the means and opportunity to murder John, of that, there was no doubt.

What I was left to wonder about was the why.

Sid had been one of the first people to try to get into the pajama factory after the ownership had changed hands. He'd been the one to suggest the property was owned by the bank and demand Tex let him in to search for evidence in a death that had long since been ruled accidental. I'd written him off as a conspiracy theorist, the kind of person who probably stood outside the Book Depository on the anniversary of JFK's death and prompted people to consider alternate theories about who shot the president in 1963, before he'd even been born.

But he'd acted truly surprised when I'd said that I now owned the building. What if he didn't know? If John hadn't told him? And that was how he found out? Would something like that make him angry enough to kill his spouse?

It all depended on how strong their marriage had been to begin with.

I'd read somewhere that divorce rates were lower in states that allowed same-sex marriages than those that did not recognize the unions. That made sense. With national divorce statistics over 50 percent, it seemed too many people rushed into marriage before they were ready. The hurdles in place for same-sex couples would be enough to make anyone think twice before making things legal. If John and Sid were married, then they thought it was worth the difficulties. That much I could assume. But what I didn't know was whether or not, a few years in, they shared that same level of commitment.

I realized I was still holding the phone with Connie on the other end, but neither of us had spoken for over a minute. "Connie? Are you still there?"

"Yes. Sorry. I put the phone down so I could get this tape straight."

"Okay, listen to me. I don't know what's going on here, but I think I know how to get answers. Can you find me an address for an organization called the Truthers?"

"Sure. Hold on."

I held the phone by my ear and watched the pajama factory. Two police cruisers had arrived since I'd been there. They were parked by the front of the property, their blue and red lights spinning a silent command for everyone to calm down. I shielded my eyes and looked for uniforms. A couple of officers stood by the group of picketers in a face-off. Neither side looked particularly aggressive, but they were each performing their tasked-out role. By the looks of things, I half expected someone from Sid's team to offer one of the cops a Pepsi.

"Got it. Are you ready?"

"Text it to me. Are you okay at the studio?"

"Sure. I booked you an appointment for a Polynesian den and somebody put down a deposit on Rocky's ball chair."

"Keep up the good work. I'll call you when I can."

The Truthers offices were a couple of blocks away from the pajama factory, so I left my car in the lot and walked. Ninety percent of my motivation was because the weather was nice and it seemed wise to let people think I was one place when I was really in another. Ten percent was to prove Tex's words about abusing my injured knee didn't bother me. Okay, maybe fifteen.

I rounded the corner at the end of the block and, with a glance of confirmation that nobody was following me, hurried forward. Two more blocks west and one block north and I stood in front a string of street-facing businesses. Despite the scent of coffee and pastries that spilled out of the bakery on the corner, I went directly to the address Connie had texted me.

The front doors to Truthers were open, but the second set of doors just inside were locked. I pressed my face against the glass and looked inside. The lights were off, but I could make out several secondhand desks and chairs and a massive file cabinet in the corner. On top of the desks were sheets of thick cardboard and markers that had probably been used in the making of the picket signs. By all accounts, it looked like a campaign office for an underdog candidate who gets by with grass roots marketing. It completely matched the image I'd picked up from Sid since meeting him that first day at the pajama factory. A wannabe hippie who'd been born in the wrong decade.

I'd met John Sweet, and putting him and Sid together in my mind didn't change my opinion of either one significantly. I could see them together just as easily as I could have pictured each of them with someone else. There were no red flags that told me the entire marriage was a sham, but there was nothing else I could see that led me down any other paths. The only things I knew at this point were that John and Sid had been married and now John was dead, and Sid was suing me for ownership of the pajama factory that had once been owned by John's grandfather.

It was a weak thread, like the rotted spools that had been left on the sewing machines. I needed more. I turned around to leave and noticed a small stack of brochures in a wall-mounted fixture. *Your Money. Our Work. Help us sleuth for your truth! Become a donor today.*

I picked up the brochure and scanned the copy. It was vague on specifics, citing only that they raised money to do good, right wrongs, and be a watchdog in the community. What wrongs had they righted? I wondered. I opened the brochure. Aside from the fancy logo, contact information, and request for funding, there wasn't much content. I closed the brochure and was about to put it into my handbag when something caught my attention. It was an acknowledgment of thanks to the gold-level donors who allowed Truthers to continue their efforts in the Deep Ellum area.

The first name on the list was Big Bro Security.

I knew who owned Big Bro Security. It was the same person who owned the silver Saab that was parked along the curb right outside the Truther offices.

Former police officer Donna Nast.

TWENTY-EIGHT

I exited the Truthers offices and pounded on Nasty's tinted car window. "Open up, Nasty. I know you're in there."

The window rolled down halfway. "Madison, you delivered this case to me on a silver platter. I should thank you."

"Send me a fruit basket."

"No, I mean it. You're so gullible. Tex would never have told me about the pajama factory or the gun. But you, you're so starved for female friendship you thought we were bonding."

I crossed my arms. "What do you think you're going to accomplish with all this? The actress you're using to get close to me should be grieving. She lost her grandmother and her brother within a week of each other. Don't you think you're taking advantage of her a little?"

"Erin has nothing to do with this."

"Yes, she does, at least a little. And you're not surprised by anything I just said. You already knew she was connected to this case. Erin didn't hire you to run security or investigate the pajama factory. She hired you to help her get a part in a movie, not to use her as a pawn in whatever you're doing to get closure on the case you screwed up that cost somebody his life."

She threw the door to her Saab open so fast it slammed into my bad knee. I jumped backward and hopped on my other foot while sparks of nerve endings exploded in my joint.

"I didn't screw up that case."

"Are you sure you believe that? Because if you did, you

wouldn't be here."

"I hate you, Madison. I hate your goofy outfits and your stupid lamps and your pink sneakers and your ugly car."

"What did I ever do to you?"

She glared at me. Her lips were pursed, making her already pronounced cheekbones stand out even further. Her hair hung over her right shoulder, the golden blonde streaks framing the side of her face. Even angry, she was gorgeous—and half my age. I searched her face for a clue and waited for an explanation of some sort. Nasty had everything, and her hostility was as big a mystery as some of the cases we'd both survived.

Neither of us spoke for several seconds. "This isn't about what you think it's about," she finally said.

She climbed back into her car and slammed the door shut. I took a few steps back just in case her anger led her to run over me. Her engine started, and her tires spun, leaving rubber tracks on the concrete as she backed out and then peeled away.

I watched her tail lights fade and then walked back toward the pajama factory while favoring my knee. Two more patrol cars had arrived, and the crowd had dispersed. I looked to the left and right for Sid but didn't see him. A pile of abandoned picket signs was stacked on the dead grass to the left of the front doors.

I called Tex. "Are you on your way?"

"I sent a couple of squad cars to handle it."

"Where are you?" He didn't say anything. "I'm not trying to be a nuisance. I need to talk to you. I'm here, at the factory, and I just had a run in with Nasty. She's—something's going on with her."

"I'm investigating a lead at the storage facility."

"Which storage facility?"

"Hernando's. The one where you found Alice's stuff."

"I can't believe you! I'm down here trying to figure things

out and you're hitting on that woman who works there, aren't you?"

"Night—"

"Don't move. I'm on my way."

Tex's Jeep sat under the pink dogwood tree in the far corner of the lot. The surrounding spaces had already been taken. Two handicap spots by the front door remained available, but ever since the doctor had proclaimed my knee injury had healed as far as it would, I'd vowed never to park in a handicap space again. I circled the lot twice, eventually pulling into a spot vacated by a motorcycle with a small stuffed teddy bear strapped to the back.

I wasn't about to make a scene, but the longer I sat in the car, the more I felt like I was wasting my time just sitting there. I went inside the front office. Rachel, the lone Hernando employee, met me with a forced smile. "Hi," she said. "Captain Allen said you would be coming. He's waiting for you by your storage locker."

"Thank you," I said. Tex was already at Alice's unit? What was he doing in there?

I drove my car through the gates and parked by the double doors, and then scaled the stairs and followed the narrow hallway to the storage unit. Tex was leaning against the wall. His eyes were closed. I spun the dial to turn on the light timer, and Tex opened his eyes.

"How come you're in here and she's out there?" I asked.

"I didn't come here for the manager."

"That young lady out there isn't the manager." I turned around and looked behind me. "Is she?"

"Assistant manager," he said. He stood up straight. "She's the reason I came here yesterday, but she's not the reason I'm here today."

"You are incorrigible."

"You wouldn't know what to do with me if I weren't." He grinned and put his phone into the pocket of his suit pants. "Now, what's the trouble with Nasty?"

"She's out of control. You know Sid, that guy who keeps showing up with picket signs to get inside the pajama factory? He's suing me. Did you know he was married to one of your victims? Nasty had to have known him, maybe even put him up to this. She's one of his donors—the donors for his non-profit."

He studied me while I spoke. The joking expression he'd worn seconds earlier was gone and in place was his cop mask. "Tell me what Nasty said. Exact words."

"I don't have a transcription. She made me mad and I returned the favor."

"Night, give me more than that."

I glared at him. Nasty's words came back to me: her calling me stupid and saying how easy it had been to play me for information. How I'd fallen for her bonding routine. I was as interested in facing any possible truth to her observations as she'd be in hearing me tell her she dressed like a cheap tart. I didn't like the prospect of sharing her observations about my shortcomings to Tex, but if it could help Tex shut her down, he needed to hear it.

"You called it. You told me Nasty only looks out for Nasty, and you were right. She was right too. I thought she was opening up to me when she told me about her case, but she was playing me to get information. I told her everything she wanted to know. God, she's right. I am stupid."

"Nasty called you stupid?"

I nodded. "She said this isn't about what I thought it was about."

"What do you think it's about?"

"The case she quit over. I think Nasty can't let go of the fact that because of her error a man killed himself."

"You told her that?" he asked. I nodded. "How'd she react?"

"She told me she hated me."

Tex's expression changed. "Hate?"

"Strong word, right? She said she hated my clothes..."

He looked at my flowered pantsuit. "Well..."

"...and my business and my sneakers and my car. What did I ever do to her?"

For a tense couple of seconds, Tex and I stared at each other. My skin went prickly, and my temperature rose. I was afraid to move, and even though a window was open at the end of the otherwise vacant hallway, it became difficult to breathe. Tex stood up, away from the wall he'd been leaning against, and closed the distance between us. He started slowly at first, but by the time he reached me, it was like the undertow of the ocean pulling us together.

He put his hands on either side of my face and kissed me. His lips felt soft against mine. It was as unexpected as Nasty's insults, but something kept me from pushing him away. My mouth opened and he nibbled on my lower lip. Surrounded by narrow storage units, with a padlock from the one on the wall opposite Alice's now pressing into my back and a flickering fluorescent tube light overhead, I forgot about everything else going on in my life and kissed him back.

Someone cleared her throat.

I pulled away from Tex and looked to my left. I was vaguely aware of Tex's hand cupping the side of my breast through the thin fabric of my lavender shirt underneath the pink princess-cut blazer.

Rachel stood in the doorway. "You, um, have been back here for a while," she said. "I wanted to make sure everything was okay." The look on her face said that everything *wasn't* okay, and that the policy on fooling around in the storage units may or may not have been the reason why. "I have to, um, get back to the front desk." She turned around and left.

"I have to go too," I said.

"Night, wait."

But I didn't. I took two steps away from Tex and then practically ran out of the storage facility. It wasn't until I was in my car and three miles away that I let myself think about what the heck had happened.

Was that what Nasty was so bent out of shape about?

TWENTY-NINE

A flood of emotions swirled together, like the base color and tint in a paint can before they're mixed. Exhaustion and hunger. Guilt. Grief. I was a ticking time bomb ready to blow and had no outlets for my stress. It was late afternoon. If I went to Mad for Mod, I'd end up telling Connie what had happened, and until I knew how I felt about the kiss, I wasn't ready to analyze it with anyone else. As long as it remained between me and Tex (and Rachel), it was a moment frozen in time. Maybe I could blame it on early menopause.

I called Connie to let her know she was on her own for the rest of the day.

"You okay, Mads?" Connie asked. "You sound funny."

"I'm okay. I'm just—there's a lot on my mind. The Mummy event and the pajama factory and a whole bunch of other things I don't want to talk about. I'll power through it like I always do. I'm just happy to have you there to help me."

"Yeah, um, about that. Well—we can talk later. No worries on closing up tonight, but you should probably call Richard. He's freaking out a little about some letter you left on his desk."

"Of course, he is. I'll handle it."

I hung up and drove home on autopilot. Would I be able to throw myself into work and forget about the kiss with Tex in the hallway of Hernando's Hide-It-Away? Did I want to? I didn't know what I was feeling about that. I didn't know how I felt about a lot of things these days, and for someone who liked to have everything just so, the sense of not knowing was one more thing that left me off-kilter.

I parked in front of the hedge and went inside. Rocky met me by the door, and I let him out. I set the now cold shrimp fried rice on the table, grabbed my cell phone, and followed Rocky into the yard.

Richard answered on the third ring. "Mummy Theater."

"Richard," I said. "It's Madison. I got a message to call you."

"When were you going to tell me you rearranged everything?" he asked.

"I didn't rearrange anything. It's exactly like it was when I was there earlier today."

"This agenda on my desk. It says 'Call Madison.'"

I watched Rocky dig a hole and then drop a pink rubber ball into it. "Did you read the agenda?"

"No. It says 'Call Madison' so I'm calling Madison. Where did this new agenda come from?"

"Richard, you and Dax were getting high in your office. Remember? I came in and told you the event was under control. I had you write down the agenda so you would recognize your handwriting and know we had that conversation. Look at the sheet of paper. Whose handwriting is that?"

"Dax's."

"No, it's not. It's yours. I watched you write it."

"Hold on," he said. I heard the phone clunk down onto the desk on his end and then a series of sounds that made me pull my own phone away from my head. Rocky ran to the garage and back, fur flying behind him. He slowed to a jog and then a walk by the time Richard returned. "Yeah, um, Dax spilled a cup of coffee on my desk. There's a crumpled and soggy version in the trash. He must have recopied the notes before they were completely ruined."

"Okay, then you're looking at an agenda for your meeting,

written in Dax's handwriting. What's the problem?"

"The problem is we always do things the same way: picnic, cocktail party, movie."

"And that's how you're doing it this time."

"Not according to this. It says right here the shuttle service is taking the managers from the picnic to your pajama factory for a fashion show before the movie showing at midnight."

Now I was annoyed. "That's not what I wrote down. I specifically made you write down that there was a picnic at the lake and then a showing of *The Pajama Game* at The Mummy."

"It's too late for that. I sent the agenda to the printers this morning. It's already a rush job. When are you coming by with the pajamas?"

"What pajamas?"

"Come on, Madison. You promised me a pajama fashion show. You have access to a whole building filled with PJs, right? Bring whatever looks like it came from the movie. Colorful, striped, His and Hers. Don't tell me they didn't make them. I saw the ad. I know that was their thing."

"That inventory is no longer available."

"Why not? Dax said the police released the crime scene."

"Where did he hear that?"

"On the news. So? What are we going to do about this?"

"We? We are going to call the printer, tell them there's a mistake on the program, cancel the job, and send a new file with the correct information."

"No."

"Richard, there is absolutely no way I'm giving permission to allow a conclave of theater managers into my factory for a pajama fashion show. Zero. The longer you stick on that point, the less time you'll have to come up with a new plan."

"I think you forget that you work for me."

"I think you forget that you don't pay me." I countered.

"Tick tock, Richard."

"Fine. Get the inventory from your factory and have the fashion show here."

I hung up the phone and said a couple of words that probably weren't in Doris Day's vocabulary. Richard's managerial manner was a lot easier to take when he was stoned, though that too required a certain level of compromise. Everything else in my life was changing. Maybe, after this event, it was time to stop volunteering at The Mummy.

It was four thirty. I heated my shrimp fried rice in the microwave and ate it quickly. If I were going to get the pajama inventory from Sweet Dreams for Richard, it would be better to do it while the sun was up than to wait for night. The police had already dealt with one event there today, and I knew Sid and his picketers had been warned away. Tex knew everything I knew at this point. And Sid's lawsuit had started a different ticking clock that meant if I didn't get the PJs right now, I probably wasn't going to get them at all.

Despite Richard's annoying direction, I looked forward to selecting samples to showcase on models at the event. On my first trip to the factory, I'd only briefly looked at the nightshirt with the colorful conversation heart print, but the cubby holes in the inventory cage were filled floor to ceiling with assorted styles: night gowns and two-piece sets, styles for summer and winter. I begrudgingly accepted that Richard's demands let me shift my attention away from the murders and onto something far more frivolous and fun.

I clipped on Rocky's leash, and we headed downtown. By the time we reached Sweet Dreams, it was after five. I parked in the lot across the street and carried Rocky to the front doors. He wriggled out of my arms when we reached the front of the building and immediately attacked the dirt in the corner of the flower beds out front while I flipped through the second set of keys I'd picked up from Stanley & Abbott until locating the one that unlocked the building.

"Come on, Rock, let's make this quick," I said.

He looked up at me with his big brown soulful eyes and whimpered. I squatted down so we were face to nose.

"I haven't paid you enough attention lately, have I? I'm sorry. You're my little man, right? And you miss Hudson's cat even if he does hiss at you and swat you in the nose." I ruffled Rocky's fur and hugged him. He stood still for a few seconds, and then wriggled free and returned to the corner of the flower bed to resume his digging. "Silly dog," I said to myself.

I stood up, flexed my knee a couple of times, and unlocked the doors to the pajama factory. I dropped the key ring into the pocket of my blazer and turned toward Rocky. He had something in his mouth. I let go of the door and stooped back down. "Whatcha got there? What did you find in the dirt?"

Whatever Rocky had dug up was still stuck in the ground. He growled and shook his head like when we played tug-of-war with his rope bone until the item that had been buried came loose and swung over his head. It landed on the sidewalk by my feet in a dull jingle.

I picked it up and shook off the dirt. It was a length of tarnished brass chain. Dangling from the chain was a small round disc stamped with the number 42 and a copper key like the one I'd just used to unlock the front door of Sweet Dreams.

THIRTY

A chill swept over me. Had this key been buried in the flower bed for the purposes of letting someone get inside to murder John Sweet?

I pulled out my phone to call Tex.

Tex. The kiss. I'd taken off and driven away, and now things would be weird. Just that thought was stupid. I was forty-nine years old. I wasn't supposed to delay calling the police because I'd kissed one of them.

I called Tex and held my phone to my ear. He answered, and I talked. Fast. "It's Madison," I said. I rushed ahead before he could get the wrong idea about why I was calling. "I found a key. Well, Rocky found a key. In the flower beds outside the pajama factory."

"You're at the pajama factory?" he asked. His voice was tense.

"You released the building, right? It was on the news."

"The building gets released to the owner. Did I contact you to tell you it was released?"

"No, but it was on the news."

Tex cursed. "Yes, the building has been released. I was going to tell you earlier today, but—"

I rushed ahead so he wouldn't talk about the kiss either. "I need to get some pajamas out of the storage cage for an event at The Mummy. They're my pajamas, and I expect to be in and out before—hold on." Rush-hour traffic from the highway drowned out the conversation, making it impossible to hear. I unlocked the door and stepped inside to block out the noise. Rocky followed. I closed the door. "I'm inside, and I'm going to get what I need and be gone before you know it. Do you want me to drop the key off at the station?"

"I'm at your place. You can give me the key when you get here."

"Why are you at my place? You didn't expect..." I'd been all mixed up, but apparently, Tex switched more easily between gears than I did. I let my voice trail off, not wanting to put into words what I was thinking.

He was silent for a moment. "Doesn't matter why I'm here. Get out of there, Night." He hung up.

Tex's tone both angered and scared me. I didn't much like being told what to do, but I couldn't escape the creepy factor of being alone in this rather large building where someone had recently been murdered. Richard could shell out for store-bought pajamas. I'd planned his whole event and rolled with the punches when he and Dax had mixed things up—assuming it had been a mix-up and not a clear effort on Dax's part to undermine me and get into the building despite my protests.

"Rocky?" I called. Where had that little dog gone? I heard a yip from across the factory floor. He peeked his head out from behind the sliding doors that separated the sewing room from the inventory and George's office. "Get over here," I demanded. He took a few steps toward me and then turned around and went back into the cage. "Rocky!" No response.

I crossed the wooden floor of the pajama factory, weaving between sewing stations. My pant legs swished against each other. The cart where I'd tossed my cookies the day Tex and I found John Sweet's body was gone. For some reason, the consideration of Tex having taken care of that tiny detail in the midst of a homicide investigation was touching, until I realized the police had likely collected the contents of the cart as evidence. I looked around the floor of the factory. The sewing machines had been stripped of their spools of thread. The other small signs that had made the factory appear to have been closed mid-workday were gone, making it look more like a ghost town than a time capsule.

I pulled my phone out and called Tex back. "Hey," I said.

"Can't get me out of your head, can you, Night?"

"You're the one waiting at my house while I go about my life."

"Are you on your way?

"No, I told you I'm at the pajama factory. I'll leave in a minute."

"I told you to get out of there."

"God! This is never going to work if you insist on telling me what to do."

The second it was out of my mouth, I froze. Had I just said that? To Tex? Had he heard me? I stood still, waiting for his response. Maybe the call had cut out. Maybe a car had driven by. Maybe he hadn't been paying attention.

When Tex spoke, his voice was emotionless and steady. "When I went to Hernando's yesterday, it was to find out who rented the storage unit. It wasn't your friend Alice. It was John Sweet."

"But John is dead. If he's behind all this, who killed him? And why? He couldn't have been working alone. He was in the factory and the front doors were locked. The key was buried. You can try to get prints off it, right? I'll bring it to you after I get the pajamas."

Tex was quiet for a moment, and this time when he spoke, his voice sounded direct. "Listen to me very carefully. We found evidence in the upper floors of the factory that someone has been living in that building. There's a very good chance the key you found buried out front is how the killer got in."

"But if the key was buried, then whoever did this had to have left."

"And when they come back, they'll know you found them out."

I looked behind me at the door to the pajama factory. I hadn't locked it when I came inside because I hadn't expected to be here for more than a minute. "Rocky's in the inventory cage. I'll be on my way in thirty seconds." I hung up and put the phone in the opposite pocket as my keys. The two weighted items bounced against my hip bones as I walked. I reached the cage and went inside. Rocky's head was buried in the bottom cubby that held men's XL pajamas in the conversation heart print.

I didn't know when this inquisitive side of Rocky had emerged or how long it was going to last, but it seemed as though all I'd been doing lately was holding him back from nosing around in things that weren't his business. The irony of that wasn't lost on me.

I tapped Rocky on his haunches. "Come on, little man, let's go home."

Rocky backed himself out of the cubicle. In doing so, the plastic bags that held the conversation heart pajamas shifted against each other and fell onto the floor with a clunk.

That was odd. Pajamas don't clunk.

I squatted on the floor and shifted the fallen bag. It wasn't filled with new old stock pajamas like the other cubicles.

Underneath the inventory were guns. Lots and lots of guns. Just like the one I'd been left in the unit at the storage facility and the one I'd seen John Sweet holding when Tex and I had found his body. And while my brain processed what it could possibly mean, I became aware of a second, more frightening sound.

Footsteps crossing the floor directly over my head.

THIRTY-ONE

Tex had told me they'd found evidence of someone living in the factory. It was information I shouldn't have had. He'd compromised his investigation to warn me so I'd leave. And I hadn't. And now here I was, hiding in an inventory cage full of vintage pajamas while a killer or gun runner—or both—approached. And worse than my terror, my fear over what was about to happen to me, was my fear for Rocky. To everybody else, he was just a dog. To me, he was family.

I'd been so sure that the presence of the key in the flower bed meant whoever might have gotten in was elsewhere, but my back had been turned away from the door when I found the key. Someone could have slipped into the factory just like I had when I'd stepped inside to get away from the noise of the traffic out front. And if they had, they would have hidden.

Had I told Tex why I was there? I couldn't think; I couldn't remember. If I'd mentioned the pajama inventory, then whoever was in the building could have waited me out. I'll be gone in thirty seconds. I said that, right? Why couldn't I think straight?

Rocky looked up at me and yipped. Another bark, fainter than the last, sounded from the door to the right. I scooped up Rocky and clamped my hand over his mouth. And listened. More sounds, coming from—where? Was another animal trapped inside the closet?

What were my options? Run for the front door with Rocky and leave another animal behind? I couldn't do that. My eyes fell on the pile of guns that had been hidden in the cubby with the conversation heart PJs. I'd be a fool to think the other person in the factory wasn't armed.

I held Rocky to my chest and backed away from the sliding doors until I was up against the desk. Slowly, I shuffled to my right. I reached out for the doorknob to the closet in the corner. If we could duck in there and lock it from the inside, we might be able to go unnoticed long enough for me to figure out a better plan.

The footsteps overhead had stopped. I could picture someone listening to see if they'd imagined Rocky's bark. But the front door was open. My car was outside. It wasn't difficult to place me right here where I was. Add in the doggy sounds and there would be no mystery to my identity. If only the opposite were true.

And then, the footsteps resumed. This time on the stairs.

The knob turned easily. I ducked inside, realizing too late I hadn't entered a closet. I'd opened the door that led down to fixture storage. I pulled the door shut behind me. My jacket caught. I stumbled for footing. Rocky squealed. I set him down on the steps and quickly opened and shut the door to free the corner of my jacket. I scampered down the stairs and crouched behind a rolling rod filled with samples of mint green and butter yellow nylon tricot peignoir sets.

The footsteps were directly over my head. Whoever was up there was headed my way. I wished I knew who it was. Who'd been behind everything? How could someone have gotten away with so much without leaving evidence behind?

Rocky ran into the corner and made happy snorting sounds. Another face, that of a small, scared Chihuahua took two steps out of the darkness. I was so surprised by the presence of a second dog that I froze. I *had* heard a bark.

Rocky had recently been enamored with a Chihuahua at

Mad for Mod. It didn't seem likely that so small of a dog could have traveled from Greenville Avenue to Deep Ellum on her own, though it was possible. But how would she have gotten into the basement of Sweet Dreams? Was there a broken window or another way in and out?

Or was someone keeping her here in the basement of the pajama factory? Someone who had been to Mad for Mod?

I closed my eyes and tried to remember the past few days. I pictured a sea of faces, all the people I'd talked to over the past week: Nasty, security company owner; Clara, sister of the victim who'd died at Sweet Dreams; Frannie, cleaning woman; Erin, wannabe actress; Rachel, storage-facility assistant manager; Sid, John's husband and Truther; Dax, historical building preservationist; Richard, theater manager. Of all the people I could remember, only one had been to Mad for Mod.

But that didn't mean anything. The Chihuahua had been alone. No tags. No leash. No owner. Anyone could have been lurking around my place of business—if indeed that's what happened. I needed something more than what I was coming up with.

I pulled my phone out a third time, but couldn't get a signal. I was in the basement of the factory, hiding amongst mannequin parts and racks of sherbet-shaded jammies. A middle-aged woman and two small dogs.

Things could have been better.

I picked Rocky up and held him in front of my face. "You have to trust me, okay?"

I spun around and searched for a place I could hide him, where he'd be safe. A large canvas bin like the ones that had held fabric on the factory floor sat alongside the far wall. I carried him to the bin and set him in the bottom. Piles of vintage fabric—satin and gingham and flannel and lace—filled the cart. Rocky quickly burrowed his way under the fabric swatches like he knew how important it was for him to stay hidden. I bent down and called out for the Chihuahua, finally cornering her. She was shaking. I scooped her up and put her in the fabric bin with Rocky. Their companionship would leave them less lonely if anything happened to me.

I turned around the small basement, scanning racks of pajamas, boxes of broken mannequin forms, and file cabinets labeled for purchase orders, sleepwear designs, and pay stubs for employees who hadn't graced the property for decades. I pulled a file out and looked inside. It was a preservationist's dream: detailed records from the operation of the pajama factory kept in pristine condition by the sheer fact of having been abandoned under an unfortunate cloud of scandal.

I thumbed through the B files and came to Clara. She'd worked at the factory for over a decade, receiving a modest increase to what looked like a paltry hourly wage each year. She'd told me the job supported her family, along with the wages of her sisters, but that they'd all agreed that Suzy was the one who had a chance to do more with her life than factory work. Maybe that's why the file on Suzy Bixby, still in the file cabinet, caught my eye.

I slid Clara's file back into place and pulled out Suzy's. Had Clara been lying about Suzy working at Sweet Dreams?

I lost all track of the footsteps over my head and the rustling sounds of the two dogs nesting in the sample bin and flipped Suzy's file open.

The first sheet of paper was a standard report from an insurance company. It detailed the malfunction of the steamer that had killed Suzy Bixby, signed by a representative from the equipment manufacturer. Behind it, clippings from newspapers both local and national wrote articles about the accident and the tragic death of the young model. Suzy's face smiled out from the images in the paper. Behind the articles was a letter from

George to the press that refused release of the recent ad campaign photos for use in articles about Suzy's death. In his own words: *This accident has led to tragedy and for Sweet Dreams to benefit from the use of a company publicity photo in reports of a local model's death would be wrong.*

The last thing in Suzy Bixby's file was a job application to work at Sweet Dreams. The word Rejected was stamped along the upper right-hand edge of the paper and initialed A. S. in the same cursive I'd seen on Alice's original letter that I'd found lying on her kitchen table. The application was dated only a few days before Suzy had died. She'd applied for a job at Sweet Dreams, and Alice had been the one to reject her application.

Suzy had no business operating the steamer at Sweet Dreams. So why had she? Was she playing around unsupervised or using the equipment for her personal needs? Had her sister Clara told her to use the steamer when no one was looking? And by doing so had she enabled and then witnessed the ensuing accident that took her sister's life?

There was no doubt to me that the courts had ruled the steamer malfunction accidental and that Sweet Dreams held no liability for the model's death. George's decision to close the factory had been his alone.

Though I'd never know what he'd been thinking, I couldn't help but wonder if he'd been caught in a cage of his own guilt, having been the father figure for so many of the young women who found employment at his factory and losing one in such a horrible way.

The floor over my head creaked, and I froze.

While my remaining questions about Suzy Bixby's death had been answered, my situation hadn't improved. I was still trapped with no way out. And no matter who it was that was upstairs, I could assume they were armed. There had been more than enough guns in the pajama cubby to riddle my body with bullets. I had mannequin parts and satin nightgowns. Not exactly a fair fight with whoever was behind this.

The police should have found those guns when they'd searched the place for evidence after finding John's body. That they hadn't indicated that someone had been coming and going, using the factory as a temporary holding location.

I stood as still as I could and listened for sounds to indicate what the other person in the factory was doing. A door shut. A key activated tumblers in a lock. The footsteps receded and then returned.

Receded and returned.

Receded and returned.

Someone was moving back and forth from above my head to the factory door.

Someone was moving the guns.

I could bide my time and let them get away with it. With who knows how many guns that would be sold illegally and cause more destruction than a hundred malfunctioning cast-iron steamers.

I couldn't let them get away with it.

I had no idea how the night was going to end for me, but I wouldn't leave Rocky's safety up to chance.

I turned my phone to silent and texted Tex: Rocky in fabric bin in basement of Sweet Dreams with another dog. Save them. No signal.

I grabbed a broken white mannequin arm from a box next to the staircase and climbed on top of a cabinet along the north side of the building. The fingers on the mannequin arm barely reached the window positioned at ground level. I tried, unsuccessfully, to reach the window's handle and undo it.

Out of desperation, I swatted the white limb against the glass several times until finally, the glass shattered. Now, relying on my high school softball pitching experience, I chucked the phone at the hole in the window, and it sailed outside.

I climbed down and carried the mannequin arm like a club up the staircase. The door to the basement opened just as I reached for the knob.

THIRTY-TWO

Erin Haney stood in front of me. She wore a full-skirted dress with matching ballerina flats. Her highlighted hair was held back by a low ponytail, and her eyes were wide. "Madison? You scared me! What were you doing down there? Why are you holding an arm?"

Erin was in Dallas to research a part in a movie. But was she? Erin had told no one about her trip to Dallas. In her own words, she'd wanted to stay off the radar. Her agent didn't know. Her family didn't know. Her older brother John, who died in this very building, didn't know. Or so she'd said.

I shook my head. Erin had been noticeably upset when Tex had delivered the news about John at Alice's house. But Erin was an actress. She'd been trained to fake things like that.

I stepped into the inventory cage and closed the basement door behind me. Erin had hired Nasty and shadowed her around Lakewood. She'd been at the police station and knew about Live Scan, and had left before any of us could question her interest in what we were doing. She had been keeping watch on Alice's house. Otherwise, she wouldn't have noticed my car sitting there overnight, leaving, and then coming back. Calling the police out to investigate would have given her an excuse to enter and hide the evidence that she'd recopied the letter from Alice. And for the life of me, I couldn't come up with a reason for her to be at the pajama factory now.

I studied her expression. She looked so innocent that I

doubted my suspicions. "I was looking for something."

"What?"

I reached into my pocket and pulled out the key that Rocky had dug up. "I found this out front. I have no idea how long it's been buried there. There's a number on it, and I know this will sound silly, but I was hoping to find a key log so I could see who it belonged to."

If she recognized the key or worried how much I knew, she didn't let on. Maybe I was wrong. Maybe I should just tell her—confide in her about the guns I'd found and the evidence Tex had said they'd found on the upper floors of the factory. If I was wrong about my suspicions, having her on my side would give us a better chance of survival should someone come after us. But still, I was wary.

"There's a key log right over here," she said. She turned, picked up a large leather book from the desk behind her, and hugged it to her chest. "It gives me the creeps back here. Let's go out front, okay?"

"Okay," I said. We walked side by side, the skirt of her dress flouncing out around her knees, my floral jacket and pants making a *thwik thwik* sound as the crinkle crepe fabric brushed against itself. Nothing about the moment felt threatening.

I needed a way to find out if I was completely wrong. And then I got an idea. "Did you get my message? Is that why you're here?"

"How could you leave me a message? You don't have my number." She set the ledger down on the corner of a sewing station and waited for my explanation.

How, indeed? "I called Nasty. I mean Donna," I said. "She knows how to get in touch with you, right? I asked her to relay it to you."

"What was the message?"

"To meet me here tonight."

"Donna knew you were coming here tonight?"

"Sure," I lied. Come on, Erin, say something that will tell me if you're the crazy one or if it's me. "I'm surprised she didn't tell you. To be honest, I thought she might come with you. I know how badly she wants to get in here."

Erin set down the book and flipped it open. She ran her finger down the numbers on the ledger until she reached the last line that had been filled in. "Here it is," she said. "According to this, your key belonged to Suzy Bixby. Do you know her?"

"Suzy? She was the model who died in the factory. That's strange, though. I heard she never worked here. Can I see that?" I asked. I reached for the book and spun it toward me. The name Susie Bixby was written on the last line of the ledger next to the number 42.

The name had been misspelled.

The entry had been written in a slightly different pen than the others.

The handwriting was a match for the address on the envelope I'd found in Alice's kitchen.

It took all of five seconds to confirm my suspicions about Erin. Unfortunately for me, it took Erin less time than that to pull out a gun.

THIRTY-THREE

"How long have you known?" Erin asked quietly.

"I figured it out when I was in the basement."

"I should have locked you down there with that stupid dog. She served her purpose of keeping you distracted. I should have turned her loose in the streets. Let this building take the blame for two more deaths. Or three? Where's your dog?"

"He's with a friend."

"Shame. What about the key log?"

"You misspelled her name. And Suzy didn't have a key. Her sister Clara said Suzy depended on her to get in during off hours."

Erin nodded slowly, like she was processing everything that had happened since she'd let me out. "I kept hearing her name associated with the factory, but it wasn't in the ledger. I thought it would be poetic, or maybe give the conspiracy hunters that one little clue that made them think there was more to her murder than a malfunctioning steamer."

"Those people are looking for the truth. Sid Krumholtz is probably watching the factory right now."

"Sid Krumholtz is out having dinner with Nasty. See, Madison, you gave yourself away too. You never called her, and she's not on her way here. You know she invested in Sid's company, right? They're having a business dinner at my suggestion, only I may have gotten the name of the restaurant wrong and sent them to two different places. That means neither one will have an alibi for tonight. Pity."

The innocent act was gone. What I saw in its place was how Erin had managed to get in here without being questioned. She was dressed as I dressed. The flat shoes, the vintage outfit, the ponytail. The gun was the only accessory that didn't fit.

"Put the mannequin arm down," Erin said.

I bent down slowly and set the appendage on the floor, and then stood with my hands up. "Do you want to do this? Take another life? The police won't stop looking for you when they find my body. I figured it out. They will too."

"They won't find your body," she said. "It'll be burned in an unfortunate fire that destroys the whole building. Including the records in the basement." She looked behind me. "Too bad there's no electricity. We could have had a reenactment of the steamer malfunction."

"And then what? You don't own the building. You can't collect the insurance."

She laughed, but the gun didn't waver. "I don't need insurance money. The only thing I need is to destroy evidence that we were here tonight. I almost wish Donna was on her way here. I could have framed her for your murder. So many people, so many possible frame-ups. It's been fun watching everybody run around doing exactly what I wanted them to do."

With two murders already committed and one looming in my near future, there was no doubt Erin was crazy. "Why did you kill Vernon Stanley and John Sweet?"

"Nobody was supposed to die. Everything was fine until John started thinking on his own. I did hear about you from my agent. When I saw your name in the will, I knew you'd be trouble. John came up with a whole plan to plant a gun in a storage locker and send you on a wild goose chase of rumors about Suzy Bixby and Grandpa George. He tricked his own partner into believing there was some great truth to expose."

"There's no truth to expose. The steamer did malfunction. I found a file with all the information downstairs. The reports about the malfunction, the equipment repairs up to that point that showed negligence on behalf of the maintenance company, and the lump sum payout George made to the Bixby family that forced him to close down the factory. He didn't have to make restitution, but he did. He couldn't bear knowing his company had been responsible for her death, so he made a private settlement and closed Sweet Dreams so nobody else could get hurt. All these years, Alice knew. She could have told the world and gotten George out from under the rumors, but she respected his wishes to keep it quiet so it didn't look like a publicity stunt."

"She was old. She knew she was going to die." Erin's detached articulation of Alice's last days was chilling. The woman in front of me wasn't interested in family or inheritance or legacy. She had no remorse for anything she'd done. It was at that moment I understood how slim my chances of surviving the night were. "She could have just kept quiet and let the family inherit what was rightfully ours and everything would have been fine. But she didn't. When you left the law firm that first day, Mr. Stanley started asking a lot of nosy questions. Apparently, he knew Gran better than any of us thought. John got scared and shot him. He called me, freaking out, but he said he could hide the gun in the storage locker he set up for you. It never occurred to him that you'd get out there before he could hide the gun. What is it with men? Why can't they ever see the big picture?"

"What did you do?"

"I told him to keep you busy to give me time to hide the gun in the locker. He just handed it over to me. That was his mistake. He got sloppy and acted on his own. I couldn't risk those kinds of mistakes. I needed time to move our inventory."

Inventory. It's how I referred to the build-up of mid-century modern knickknacks, accessories, and furniture I acquired at estate sales and kept in storage. It's how I thought of the bags of pajamas that were organized by size and stacked in the cubby holes by the desk.

It was how Erin Haney referred to guns. Guns that, if put into the wrong hands, would kill people.

There'd been guns everywhere I looked: one in Alice's storage locker, one in John Sweet's hand, one involved in Nasty's DUI, and a whole bunch hidden in a bag underneath the men's XL pajamas with the conversation heart print. Not to mention the one pointed at me now.

"You're trafficking in guns," I said.

"Not a bad way to make a living," Erin said casually. "Though I do owe some credit to John. He found out his boss was running guns and got in on the action."

"I don't believe for a second that Mr. Stanley was running guns."

"Not him, the other one. Mr. Abbott. Apparently for years too. John found out when one of Mr. Abbott's clients got busted by Nasty for drunk driving and she saw the gun in his car. I was here visiting John and we got the idea together."

"John killed Don Abbott? And made it look like a suicide?"

"I pulled the trigger. John wrote the note. That was the only way to be sure we could trust each other. He had access to Don's letterhead and could fake his handwriting."

"Is that where you got the idea to fake Alice's letter to me?"

She nodded. "She came to John with a will already written and asked him to execute it. That's how we learned about this place. I struck up a pen pal relationship with Grandma—excuse me—step-grandma. I thought being family would mean something."

"You thought she'd change her mind and leave Sweet Dreams to you."

"She should have. What are you to her? Captain of the old person's swim team?"

I didn't answer. I tried to remember the order of events from the day Tex and I had found John's body.

"John shot Mr. Stanley. He wanted to hide the gun in my storage locker but you knew if I got there before the gun was planted, I'd know what happened. You told him to get me to plan Alice's memorial—keep me busy—to give you time."

"I'll give you credit. You're half right."

"I'm not finished. You—you didn't want any loose ends so you planned to meet John here and you shot him. Only you'd already locked up the gun he used to kill Mr. Stanley, so you had to use a second gun. You tried to make it look like John killed himself after killing Mr. Stanley but you got sloppy when you dropped shell casings."

"John was never supposed to kill Vernon. Who do you think was going to take the fall for all this? We needed a scapegoat and we had enough on his dead partner to frame him. But John lacked focus. He let little things distract him. You know what I mean?"

I slowly moved my head from side to side.

"The only thing that mattered was keeping our stash of guns hidden. That was all. But Vernon Stanley accused John of being involved with something shady and John panicked. Instead of worrying about the guns, he worried about getting caught and shot his boss. Good thing I can think on my feet. You've been to the law firm multiple times. You even sent the cleaning woman in to find his body. You were the perfect person to frame."

"Vernon Stanley didn't need to die. He was an innocent man."

"Oh, Madison. Just when I thought you were smart." She pointed toward the stairs with her gun. "I don't have time to catch you up on everything. What does it matter anyway? You're going to die too. I always finish what I start." She tapped her temple with the hand holding the gun. "I have focus."

"There will be evidence," I said.

She pointed the gun back at me. "Of what? You being here? Sure. You were here two weeks ago. Besides, you called Captain Allen and told him you were here tonight. Evidence of the gunshot? The police already know a gun was shot in here. Getting rid of you is going to be easier than I thought. Now turn around and walk."

I still had my hands up. I lowered them. "Keep them where I can see them," Erin said. She kept the gun leveled at me. It didn't flinch; it didn't shake.

She had focus.

I walked as slowly as I could across the worn factory floor, favoring my bad knee even though I was experiencing no pain. It allowed me time to think. Erin knew what she did about me from research done by a Hollywood studio. She might think I lacked the strength to fight. I might be able to use that to my advantage.

But she knew there was something I'd missed. My mind was racing with questions she hadn't answered. I pushed them aside. The only thing I needed to worry about right now was getting away from her.

I scanned the interior of the factory ahead of me. We were weaving our way between vacated sewing stations that had been stripped down thanks to the crime-scene investigation. How I wished for a pair of scissors! To my left sat the iron steamer that had caused Suzy Bixby's death. Even if there were electricity in the building, the steamer would be of no use. It had been out of operation for over half a century. It was a dinosaur, a relic of what once was.

I didn't know how tonight was going to end, but I didn't

want to die without answers. I didn't want to die, period, but somehow, not knowing, not having any control over the situation, not being able to protect the legacy of the building Alice had kept secret all these years made everything worse. I thought about the people I'd met since being told I'd inherited the building, about what I'd learned from Nasty, from Tex, and from Erin herself since Alice had died, and a picture emerged.

I stopped walking and almost immediately felt Erin's gun in my back a few inches below the hook of my bra. "You were hiding the guns here, but after you shot John, you got them out. The police went over the factory for evidence. You thought you'd be in the clear after they released the building to me. You were going to let me come and go and if anything turned up—anything suspicious at all—you were going to use me."

"This place was perfect for what we needed. It would have worked too, if Gran hadn't had her own little secret."

"Vernon. That's it, isn't it? That's why he was so surprised that first day when I told him why I was there. He recognized Alice's name. You never expected him to pay attention to what you and John were doing, but he did. Because of their friendship."

"Affair was more like it. No wonder my grandpa chased the models who worked here. Alice didn't deserve him."

My hand flew out and slapped Erin across the cheek. I was almost more surprised than she was. Almost. Caught off guard, she dropped her gun and put her hand on her face. I kicked the gun. It skidded across the factory floor, disappearing under the inoperable iron steamer.

Erin cursed. She reached out for my head with her fingers splayed like claws and grabbed my ponytails. She yanked my head down. I closed my eyes and turned my head at the last minute. Her raised knee connected with my cheekbone. Bright spots of stars appeared in front of me and I stumbled a few steps to find my footing. My brain shouted out commands: Run. Hide. Flee. Escape. I couldn't outrun a bullet, but I had a chance to outrun Erin now that she was unarmed.

I turned away. The door was fifteen feet ahead of me. I ran. Erin tackled me. I fell. The seam on my jacket tore. My arms broke my fall. I turned over and kicked at her with my pink sneakers. Guttural sounds came out of my throat. My vision blurred from tears and dizziness, but I couldn't stop fighting against her, even after she stopped fighting back.

Strong arms wrapped around me from behind and lifted me from the floor. I struggled against them. A voice spoke in my ear.

"Night. Calm down. I'm here. She can't hurt you anymore."

It was Tex. He'd seen a raw, uncontrolled side of me. Through choked breaths, I said, "Rocky and another dog. In the basement downstairs."

"They're safe. I got your text," he whispered against my hair. "It's going to be okay."

The fight left me. I turned around and laid my head against his chest. I vaguely remembered my tears drenching his shirt before everything around me went dark.

THIRTY-FOUR

The general managers' event at The Mummy happened without my inventory or my help. I didn't care. I'd seen things that I hadn't thought existed in my town. I'd come face to face with a particular evil that had been functioning off the grid for years and that knowledge changed everything. I sent a letter to the historical preservation society expressing my interest in restoring the building for use as a shared workspace for female entrepreneurs in Dallas and copied Dax Fosse. I didn't expect their support, but I wouldn't have minded their blessing.

After learning what had happened through his Truther tip line, Sid dropped his lawsuit. I told him my plans and extended an open invitation for him to tour Sweet Dreams once the police allowed me back in. My desire to live an independent life without the possibility of emotional connection or pain dissolved. Alice's death—and the life she'd lived that I hadn't learned of until after she'd died—had shown me what I wanted out of my own life more than any emotional pain from my past could have done.

I learned that Vernon Stanley had no surviving family. When the coroner released his body, I arranged for him to be buried in the vacant plot next to Alice. I had the bare-bones tombstone that John had placed on Alice's grave replaced with a new one. *Alice Sweet 1932-2018. Sweet Dreams, my friend.*

I spent the following week getting up to let Rocky outside, sitting on the porch while he ran off his excess energy, and going back inside. I asked Connie if she'd work full-time hours while I took an unscheduled vacation. She agreed. The direction of my future was in my own hands. It was time to choose a lane.

Four days in, she called with both good news and bad: her Etsy shop had taken off and demand outweighed supply. Being the friend and professional she was, she offered me two weeks' notice. I thanked her, shortened it to one, and offered her space in my showroom to set up a workshop as a thank you for all she'd done.

I dressed in a white twinset and red pedal pushers, tied on a pair of red Keds, and took Rocky for a walk around the block. There was a note on my door when we returned. It was from the same person who had left sixteen messages on my phone. Maybe it was time to call him back.

"Night," Tex answered.

"Captain."

"I've got this spare bedroom," he said as if we'd been in the middle of a conversation, "and I don't know what to do with it. I end up closing the door, but what's the point of having a spare bedroom if you don't use it, right?"

"Spare bedroom. Right," I said.

"But, see, I'm a cop, not a decorator," he continued. "I know I could go to Bed Bath and Beyond and buy something with Martha Stewart's name on it, but that sounds like a cop out. No pun intended."

"Of course not."

"I started thinking if only I knew a decorator..."

"If only," I said. I seemed capable of contributing only the most rudimentary bits of dialogue to the conversation.

"Then I thought of you. I know you, right? And you're a decorator. Maybe I could hire you."

"Maybe you could hire me."

"Listen, Night. You're a big ball of stress. And I think I

know you well enough to know you don't want to take it out on a target in a firing range and to be honest, I don't know if I want to be in the room right now if somebody handed you a gun."

"Could I order a transcript of this conversation? You know, capture the moment so I can revisit it from time to time."

"On one condition. The next time your doorbell rings, you answer it."

"Fine." I admit, I wasn't particularly surprised when the doorbell rang.

Tex stood on the landing outside my solarium. He wore a red polo shirt and jeans. It was bright enough that he should have been wearing sunglasses but wasn't.

"What a surprise," I said.

"You busy? I want to talk to you about a decorating job."

"You have seen *Pillow Talk*, haven't you? I'm not above hot pink, tassels, and leopard print."

"Just shut up and come with me."

"I'm bringing Rocky."

"If you think you need a chaperone, that's on you."

We climbed into his Jeep. He drove to Highway 75 and exited by Oak Lawn. We were headed toward the cemetery. Twice I asked where we were going. He ignored me and kept his eyes on the road. He turned off State Street onto an alley that ran between two sets of townhouses and aimed his remote at the garage door at the end of the row. The door opened and he pulled inside.

I'd never been to Tex's house. For all the times I'd been at Greenwood Cemetery to visit Alice, I'd never known he lived less than a block away.

The garage doors closed behind us. Tex got out and went inside. Rocky and I followed. The door opened onto a narrow hallway that held a stacked washer and dryer. We passed the appliances and went up a flight of stairs that delivered us to a kitchen and living room.

I absorbed the surroundings. Tex's townhouse was a study in early aughts bachelor: marble counters in the kitchen. Black leather recliners, a big screen TV in the living room. Entertainment console with hard-wired speakers, Blu-Ray player, and a gaming device. A small furry face that looked suspiciously like Rocky's friend, the Chihuahua, peeked around the corner of the sofa. When Rocky saw her, he charged across the room. The Chihuahua pranced out from behind the sofa and the two of them sniffed each other's butts. "Keep it moving," Tex said. He tapped my behind and I glared at him. "I think we should give them their privacy."

I went up another flight of stairs and stopped on the second-floor landing. Ahead of me was a closed door. Tex reached past me and opened it. Inside was an empty room with a drop cloth on the floor, a pile of paint trays and rollers, and an assortment of paint from the collection I'd endorsed at Paintin' Place last year.

"Is this because you feel sorry for me?" I asked.

"For what? You're smart. You're alive. You might look like a cream puff, but from what I've seen, you'll probably outlive us all."

I scanned the room, taking in the natural light on the south corner and the wall that was half covered in primer. "You started without me."

"I was hoping you'd get here eventually."

I walked to the center of the room and turned, so I was facing him. I wasn't sure what I wanted to say or whether I could convey my thoughts if I found the words. "Everybody's moved on but me," I finally said.

"Maybe there's a reason for that." Tex joined me in the middle of the drop cloth and reached for my hand. I pulled away. "Calm down, Night. I'm not going to hurt you."

I tried to relax. He held his hand palm-side up and I placed my hand in his. He gently tickled the middle of my palm. The gesture felt more intimate than the kiss in the storage-unit hallway. My fingers straightened out as he flattened his palm against mine. I felt the heat from his touch in parts of my body that were nowhere near my hand.

"I'm pretty sure I know where I stand on all this. It's taken me a long time to get here, but I like where I'm at."

"You're not talking about being captain, are you?" I asked.

He shook his head. "Listen, Night. I know you're in a relationship with James, and another man might leave it at that. But there's something here. I know it and I think you know it." He paused for a moment. "Remember what I said when you asked me why I went for captain?"

"You said it was the next logical step." I didn't say it out loud, but I also remembered I'd thought the same thing about my relationship with Hudson.

We were quiet for a moment. Tex caught the tips of my fingers between his thumb and forefinger and held for a moment. "Will you do me a favor?" he asked.

"Maybe."

He smiled. "Let me know when you get tired of doing the logical thing."

Diane Vallere

After two decades working for a top luxury retailer, Diane Vallere traded fashion accessories for accessories to murder. *The Pajama Frame*, #5 in her Madison Night Mad for Mod Mystery Series, came out February 2018. She also writes the Samantha Kidd, Lefty Award-nominated Material Witness and Costume Shop, and Sylvia Stryker Outer Space mysteries. She started her own detective agency at age ten and has maintained a passion for shoes, clues, and clothes ever since.

**The Madison Night Mystery Series
by Diane Vallere**

Novels

PILLOW STALK (#1)
THAT TOUCH OF INK (#2)
WITH VICS YOU GET EGGROLL (#3)
THE DECORATOR WHO KNEW TOO MUCH (#4)
THE PAJAMA FRAME (#5)

Novellas

MIDNIGHT ICE

Henery Press Mystery Books

And finally, before you go...
Here are a few other mysteries
you might enjoy:

NUN TOO SOON

Alice Loweecey

A Giulia Driscoll Mystery (#1)

Giulia Falcone-Driscoll has just taken on her first impossible client: The Silk Tie Killer. He's hired Driscoll Investigations to prove his innocence with only thirteen days to accomplish it. Everyone in town is sure Roger Fitch strangled his girlfriend with one of his silk neckties. On top of all that, her assistant's first baby is due any second, her scary smart admin still doesn't relate well to humans, and her police detective husband insists her client is guilty.

Giulia's ownership of Driscoll Investigations hasn't changed her passion for justice from her convent years. But the more dirt she digs up, the more she's worried her efforts will help a murderer escape. As the client accuses DI of dragging its heels on purpose, Giulia thinks The Silk Tie Killer might be choosing one of his ties for her own neck.

Available at booksellers nationwide and online

Visit www.henerypress.com for details

MURDER IN G MAJOR

Alexia Gordon

A Gethsemane Brown Mystery (#1)

With few other options, African-American classical musician Gethsemane Brown accepts a less-than-ideal position turning a group of rowdy schoolboys into an award-winning orchestra. Stranded without luggage or money in the Irish countryside, she figures any job is better than none. The perk? Housesitting a lovely cliffside cottage. The catch? The ghost of the cottage's murdered owner haunts the place. Falsely accused of killing his wife (and himself), he begs Gethsemane to clear his name so he can rest in peace.

Gethsemane's reluctant investigation provokes a dormant killer and she soon finds herself in grave danger. As Gethsemane races to prevent a deadly encore, will she uncover the truth or star in her own farewell performance?

Available at booksellers nationwide and online

Visit www.henerypress.com for details

THE SEMESTER OF OUR DISCONTENT

Cynthia Kuhn

A Lila Maclean Academic Mystery (#1)

English professor Lila Maclean is thrilled about her new job at prestigious Stonedale University, until she finds one of her colleagues dead. She soon learns that everyone, from the chancellor to the detective working the case, believes Lila—or someone she is protecting—may be responsible for the horrific event, so she assigns herself the task of identifying the killer.

Putting her scholarly skills to the test, Lila gathers evidence, but her search is complicated by an unexpected nemesis, a suspicious investigator, and an ominous secret society. Rather than earning an "A" for effort, she receives a threat featuring the mysterious emblem and must act quickly to avoid failing her assignment...and becoming the next victim.

Available at booksellers nationwide and online

Visit www.henerypress.com for details

FINDING SKY

Susan O'Brien

A Nicki Valentine Mystery

Suburban widow and P.I. in training Nicki Valentine can barely keep track of her two kids, never mind anyone else. But when her best friend's adoption plan is jeopardized by the young birth mother's disappearance, Nicki is persuaded to help. Nearly everyone else believes the teenager ran away, but Nicki trusts her BFF's judgment, and the feeling is mutual.

The case leads where few moms go (teen parties, gang shootings) and places they can't avoid (preschool parties, OB-GYNs' offices). Nicki has everything to lose and much to gain—like the attention of her unnervingly hot P.I. instructor. Thankfully, Nicki is armed with her pesky conscience, occasional babysitters, a fully stocked minivan, and nature's best defense system: women's intuition.

Available at booksellers nationwide and online

Visit www.henerypress.com for details

Made in the USA
San Bernardino, CA
15 June 2020